The Bay of Marseilles and Other Stories

The Bay of
Marseilles
and Other Stories

Greg Herriges

SERVING HOUSE BOOKS

The Bay of Marseilles and Other Stories

ISBN: 978-0-9826921-9-6

Cover Art: Paul Cézanne, French, 1839-1906, The Bay of Marseilles, Seen from L'Estaque, c. 1885,Oil on canvas, 31 5/8 x 39 5/8 in. (80.2 x 100.6 cm), Mr. and Mrs. Martin A. Ryerson Collection, 1933.1116, The Art Institute of Chicago. Photography © The Art Institute of Chicago.

Author photo by Carmen Perez

Serving House Books logo by Barry Lereng Wilmont

The author wishes to extend his deepest thanks to Thomas E. Kennedy, Walter Cummins, and Rick Vittenson for editing and guidance.

Published by Serving House Books, LLC
Copenhagen and Florham Park, NJ

www.servinghousebooks.com

First Serving House Books Edition 2011

For Jeremy and Heather

with love

Also by Greg Herriges:

Someplace Safe

Secondary Attachments

The Winter Dance Party Murders

JD: A Memoir of a Time and a Journey

Streethearts

Lennon and Me

"The truth is, we know so little about life
we really don't know what the good news is
and what the bad news is."

—Kurt Vonnegut

Contents

The Bay of Marseilles
Seen from L'Estaque

He walked from one end of the arrival-departure hall to the other, hands shoved into the pockets of his newly purchased Armani raincoat. A blur of strangers moved around him as he checked from time to time the arrival monitor above the gateways. His fingers stumbled across a piece of cardboard in his right pocket. He took it out. The coat had been inspected by number thirty-eight. He wondered who thirty-eight was, pictured a woman seated at a long conveyer belt, stuffing her anonymous number in coat after coat, like messages in bottles. He went to throw the cardboard away, but changed his mind at the last second and returned it to his pocket.

An automated announcer's voice murmured something imprecise, echoed robotically through the cavernous corridors of Chicago's Union Station. The man glanced at his watch. Eleven forty-seven. He took a deep breath and felt a nervous jolt of anticipation. The cool fall air blew in from the train ports, tinged with the acrid scent of diesel fuel as a baby's stabbing cries rose and then faded in the unremitting din, the sounds of travel, of people on the move.

Her face emerged from a cluster of pedestrians marching between two steel-gray, stationary trains. He remembered the last time he had seen her, just about a year ago in this very same place, recalled the lift he had felt then as he picked her out of the crowd, the warm sensation that he sometimes enjoyed whenever he secretly thought of her.

"Darling," she said, embracing him with one arm, the other encumbered with a purse.

He whispered, "Amanda," close to her ear, held her tightly for a moment, before they joined the sea of moving bodies.

"Have you been waiting long for me?"

"Not at all. Just arrived."

"It's the most glorious weather," she said. "I tried to read a book, but I couldn't take my eyes off the trees. I've never seen such color."

She had kept her petite figure, her beauty barely muted by the passage of years. He walked proudly with her, her arm draped in his, felt a slight tug now and then as she underscored a word, a phrase, or a sudden and unexpected smile that seemed meant just for him.

"It's good to see you," he said, as they walked past a cocktail lounge, and out into the historic rotunda and past a dry cleaners.

She beamed up at him and pressed his arm with her fingers.

Out on Canal Street the clamor of traffic filled the air. It was a clear blue October day, the sun glinting off the tinted windows of skyscrapers that stood at attention in jagged rows along the lake shore.

"All the way here I thought about that little place we ate at last time. You know, the one that had the fabulous sushi."

"It's gone," he said.

"Oh—*what* a shame. I've been thinking about it and thinking about it, and now I'm famished."

"It's not the only restaurant in town, you know."

"But I was so looking forward to it."

He wanted to lean down and kiss her face, but thought better of it. It had been a year since he had last done that, and it had brought the day to an awkward halt. A trace of second-hand smoke wafted from a stopped cab, and he recalled what it had been like to smoke cigarettes in the fall.

The wind whipped across the river and felt cool against their faces as they walked down Jackson Boulevard. To the north, the Adams Street Bridge bustled with commuters and taxis and three flags waved in the breeze near the watchtower like billowing sentinels.

"It's very exciting, the city," she said. "I forget what it's like, all the movement and energy."

"On a daily basis, it can be daunting."

"Don't let's be daunted today. I only get to do this once a year. It's exhilarating."

She reached down and squeezed his hand, and he wrapped it firmly around hers. They walked briskly among the throngs to Wacker Drive, and then north all the way to Washington Street. At times he would clandestinely catch a reflection of them in shop windows, hand-in-hand, her auburn hair wisping in the wind, draped over the shoulders of her tailored leather coat. He wondered what people thought when they saw them, a couple on a stroll on a crisp autumn day. Would they think that they were in love? Married, perhaps?

"Do you remember?" she said. "We used to walk like this uptown after final exams in high school, when they gave us the afternoon off."

"I remember," he said. It was so long ago. He had difficulty believing he was with the same girl again, a woman now, all these years later. He felt a furtive thrill at the thought of it. "We used to go to Ruby's and have burgers and cokes."

"It was such a wonderful feeling, the two of us being together, I mean."

"That, and being young."

"God, we were young."

"Weren't we?"

"God."

At Dearborn they got held up at the corner as motorists continued to turn left in front of them.

"Couple of the year," he said, as the crowd pressed forward. "We were quite an item."

"Yes, we were."

"At least for a while," he said, only this time the woman did not answer him. They walked on down Washington Street among the bustling people and messengers on bicycles, her hand wrapped tightly around the sleeve of his coat. Then abruptly he added, "Your parents—"

"You can't blame them, considering."

"We're here," he said.

The Atwood Café was crammed full, but they managed to get a tiny table nudged up against a window overlooking State Street.

Sunshine sparkled off of navy blue water glasses on tables covered by cream-colored linen cloths. A pretty waitress handed them menus, said her name was Sheila, and wondered if they would like something to drink.

"Champagne," he said.

"Darling," she said, slipping out of her coat. "It's only just past noon."

"Don't listen to her," he said to the waitress. "She's from Wisconsin. We'll have a bottle of Moët and Chandon."

The waitress said very good, scribbled something on the check, and was soon lost in the crowded dining room.

"We have champagne in Portage, too, you know."

"Really?" he said, "I thought Portage was dry."

"You're such a snob. That's what comes of living on the North Shore and working in the big city. You think everybody else is from the sticks."

"No, I like the sticks. It must be very nice living in them."

"It is. It's peaceful."

"I'll bet."

"Well, it is. It's a nice place to raise . . ." she said, without finishing her thought.

"To raise what?"

"It's a nice place to live," she said.

He glanced at the menu, distracted for a moment by a woman who was staring at them. She looked familiar. Did he know her?

"How is everyone, by the way?" he asked.

She had just sipped from her water glass and took a little time swallowing. She tapped her lips gently with her napkin. "Everyone is fine. Laurie's getting so tall I almost have to look up at her. Would you like to see a picture?"

"Sure. What did you tell Michael you'd be doing today?"

She stopped short while riffling through her purse. "Are we going to start talking nonsense?"

"Not at all. I just wondered—"

"What did you tell Kate, for that matter?"

"I told her I was taking a client to lunch."

She smiled and took a finely stitched leather wallet from her purse and pulled a photo from it. "So I'm a *client*, now," she said.

"Well, I couldn't very well say, 'I'm having a day on the town with my old flame from high school.' That wouldn't go over so well."

She slid the photo across the table. A tall, thin girl atop a saddled horse looked out past him, expressionless. "You wouldn't have to mention any of that old flame stuff."

"She's very pretty," he said. "Hell of a pretty kid. She takes after her mother."

"She's a dead ringer for Michael and you know it."

"What did you tell him?"

She sighed an exasperated little sigh. "I told him I was meeting Cheryl for lunch in Chicago, and that we were going to go to Bloomingdale's afterward. Satisfied?"

"You lied."

"I *didn't* lie. I just said Cheryl instead of you, is all. Do you have a photo of William? How's he doing?"

He reached for his wallet and opened it. "He's going to be eight in two weeks. He's taking Shotokan karate lessons twice a week. He's the Karate Kid."

He handed her the photograph.

She smiled, and he remembered the little creases at the outer edges of her eyes when she did. "He's absolutely lovely. He does look like you."

"You don't say lovely for a boy."

"Well, he is and I don't care."

The waitress set two glasses before them and expertly opened the bottle, muffling the pop. As she filled the glasses, first the woman's and then the man's, she asked if they were ready to order.

"We have to toast first," he said, raising his glass.

"What should we toast?" she said.

"To Sheila, and to a wonderful autumn day in Chicago for two old flames."

She clinked her glass against his and looked at him over the rim

15

as she sipped. There were the smile creases again, just the way they had been back in high school. It was as if the day were somehow suspended, juxtaposed beside all those other days from another time, another life.

Outside a parade of passersby obediently halted as a traffic light changed. The woman regarded them distractedly. "It's beautiful," she said.

"What is?"

"The day. What shall we do with it?"

The man turned his champagne glass in circles upon the tablecloth. "I thought you said we were going to Bloomingdale's."

"That's just what I told Michael because that's what I'd do if I were with Cheryl."

"I forgot. I'm not Cheryl."

"*I* know. The Art Institute. They have that fabulous painting I remember from humanities class. What's it called—*France in the Rain*, by what's-his-name. The French painter."

"Oh—that guy. He's overrated."

"You know who I mean."

"I haven't the faintest idea."

"That's because you don't know art. But can we do it?"

He lifted his glass toward her. "Of course. Here's to what's-his-name, the French guy."

"I mean, have we time? I have to make the six-eighteen."

"We have the whole day ahead of us." Outside a street mime was drawing a crowd. He was trapped inside a predictable invisible box. "Besides, what's so important about the six-eighteen?"

The woman drew a small compact from her purse and examined her lipstick. "It's the last train to Portage, and I absolutely must be on it."

The man held his champagne glass, but did not sip from it. "Yes, it would be terrible if you missed it."

Her eyes narrowed to slits. "Don't start."

"I'm not."

"Don't even kid about it."

"Have another glass of champagne. This stuff is wonderful."

"It is, isn't it? Oh, everything is. It's a wonderful day."

"I'll drink to that." They clinked their glasses once more as a city bus roared past, blotting the sunshine with a momentary shadow that slid across the room.

He led her, his arm around her waist, through a moving quilt of pedestrians on South Michigan Avenue, past restaurants and elegant shops to the curbside crossing. The light had turned red and they waited in a crowd that slowly grew around them.

"I love the lions," she said, pointing at one of the two huge statues. "I've always loved the lions."

"Do you know what they're made of?" the man asked.

"Copper? They look like copper anyway, the way they're green and all."

"Bronze," he said.

"I didn't know bronze turned green." She stood on tiptoe to see over the shoulder of a man in a cloth coat who had stood in front of her. "How do you know, anyway?"

"I know all about the lions."

She stepped aside from him, looked up at his face doubtfully. "You're making this up, aren't you? And all because I said you don't know anything about art."

The light changed and the crowd lurched ahead.

The man grabbed her hand as they moved into the street. "They were made by Edward Kemeys. And they really are bronze."

"I don't believe you," she said, as they reached the other side of the street and began ascending the steps of the Art Institute.

"It's the absolute truth. You know I never lie."

"Like fun."

"There's more if you want to hear it."

"Such as?"

"Well, those are some pretty old lions, I'll have you know. They're from eighteen ninety-four."

"You just happen to know that."

"Yes." He reached for his wallet in his back pocket and took out two bills as they approached one of several cashiers behind a gray

17

counter. And then to the cashier: "Two adults, please."

"*There's* a slight exaggeration," she said, nudging his arm playfully.

"You're just sore because I knew about the lions."

"I still don't believe a word of it. Do ask her about the painting—you know, *France in the Rain.*"

The cashier shrugged and said that she did not know. She suggested they take a brochure from a stand.

They walked side by side past suits of armor as the woman unfolded and read a booklet, limning the lines of small print with the freshly manicured nail of her forefinger. She did not notice how the man studied the contours of her face, her upturned nose, the sensual curl of her lips. When she turned toward him she flinched slightly when their eyes met at such close proximity.

"Darling, you startled me."

"I'm sorry."

She looked around, and then back at him. "Is there something wrong? Is my makeup—?"

"Your makeup's fine. I just can't take my eyes off of you, is all."

She slapped the brochure against his chest. "Oh, now you're talking nonsense again and I don't know the artist's name. I'm going to ask a guard or a guide or somebody. Wait for me."

The painting was not *France in the Rain*, but rather *Paris Street; Rainy Day*, 1877, by Gustave Caillebotte. In the foreground a man in top hat and overcoat holds an umbrella providing shelter from the rain for both him and a fashionably dressed woman on his arm. They are walking on a broad bricked street not far from the Gare Saint-Lazare, a train station.

"It's exactly the way I remember it," the woman said. "The street looks so slippery it could be real rain. That couple, that could be us."

The man held his jacket open, hands poised upon his hips. "Yes, it could, if we were in Paris, and if it was rainy, in eighteen-seventy-seven. Of course, you'd never make the six-eighteen."

"Don't even say that," the woman scolded.

"Pardon me," the man said. "It was a joke. It just so happens we're in Chicago and it's two-thousand and ten, and it's not raining. She does sort of look like you, though."

"He doesn't look at all like you."

"I could grow a mustache. Gain thirty pounds. Get a top hat."

"Please don't."

This time he did recognize someone, a tall man in a tweed coat. He brusquely seized the woman's arm and guided her into the next room.

"What on earth?" she said.

He continued to maneuver her past and around groups of people, people admiring paintings, people speaking on cell phones, people strolling as though out for walks.

"Dick Beemis," he said by way of explanation. "He lives down the block from us. What the hell is he doing here, anyway?"

"Perhaps he likes art. Did he see you?"

"I don't know. He's so annoying."

"What's so annoying about him?" she asked.

"Always turning up when you don't need him. Let's keep walking."

He wondered if Dick Beemis had seen him, and what difference it would make if Kate found out he had been seen walking in the Art Institute with another woman. He thought about Amanda and all the years they had spent apart. The day had suddenly begun to slip away from him. Everything he had wanted to say and do, left unsaid and undone.

They wandered further into another room, and there, amongst canvasses he could neither identify nor completely appreciate, he halted as though held in place. The bluest blue and coolest aquamarine he had ever seen held him transfixed. Sun-soaked ochre houses stood one against the other, surrounding the sea, their brown and reddened roofs beveled, slanted, defying the two dimensions in which they had been rendered, playing between shadow and light, and in the background far away, rolling mountains rimmed the bay, completing a combined effect of absolute beauty and tranquility.

"What is it, darling?" she asked.

Her face before the painting of the bay made it certain for him, that there was beauty in the world, that he had missed out on it, allowed it somehow to disappear, and in contrast, the life he was living, drab, colorless. All this, but he had no words for any of it, and so he kissed her. He gathered her up in his arms and kissed her right there in front of the Cézanne and all the strangers—the millers about, the students, connoisseurs, everyone.

As their lips parted, she whispered, "What about Dick Beemis?"

"Let him find his own girl."

She unfolded herself from his embrace and led him discreetly by the hand toward an exit. Upon reaching a vestibule she turned back, asking, "Take me somewhere?"

"Sure. Sure, I'll get a cab."

"No," she said, still clinging to his hand, "don't leave me alone. I'll go with you."

There was a string of cabs curbside and the man led her down the steps one at a time, holding her forearm firmly, opening the cab door for her.

"One sixty Pearson," he said to the driver.

The taxi listed into traffic, nudging her close against his side.

After a little while she said, "What brought that on back there?"

He looked uncertainly at her. "I don't know. I just realized how beautiful you were, I guess. Not just you, the moment. Moments don't last. You know how it is—they're there, and then they're gone. Then all you can do is remember them. I was just trying to hold on to that one, make it last."

She dabbed her eyes with an inch or so of the cuff of her blouse that showed beneath the sleeve of her leather jacket.

"Did I upset you?"

"No," she sniffled as she spoke. "Don't be silly. It was lovely. I need a drink, is all."

"We just had champagne."

"I know. I need a real drink now. Where are you taking me?"

It was the twelfth floor of the Ritz Carlton, an art-deco lobby under a translucent greenhouse ceiling. They chose two upholstered chairs tucked away in an alcove, a coffee table before them.

"Am I dressed for this?" the woman asked.

"It's casually elegant—just like you."

"God," she said, taking off her leather jacket, "I feel like an ad for America's Dairyland all of a sudden."

A young waiter in a starched white shirt and perfectly creased black trousers approached them, asked if they would care for anything to drink.

"Vodka and cranberry. Belvedere, if you have it," the woman said.

"And for you, sir?"

"Ah—Johnnie Walker, Black Label, on the rocks."

The young man went off with their drink order while cool jazz played from invisible speakers and well-dressed people filled the open space. The man took one of her hands in both of his. "If anything I did today caused you to be upset—"

"It isn't anything you said or did. It's just that it's always just below the surface, and sometimes it's harder to keep it down there. Like just a while ago, in front of the Cézanne."

"The what?"

"The painting," she said.

"The one with the blue water?"

"Yes, the artist's name—it's Cézanne. You really don't know art, do you?"

"It's just that I'm not used to seeing things like that, in that way. And then seeing you in front of it, as beautiful as ever—"

"Shh. You're doing it again."

The young waiter returned with their drinks and placed each upon a little coaster on the table in front of them. "Can I get you anything else right now?"

"No, thank you," the man said.

As the waiter walked away she said, "Doesn't he look like the boy in *La Bamba*?"

"La what?"

"*La Bamba*. The boy who went down in the plane, I mean."

"I don't know."

They both sipped from their drinks. The man removed his trench coat and folded it on the back of his chair. Beneath his shined oxford shoes was a damask carpet, the shade of autumn leaves.

"We have others to think about," the woman went on, as if continuing an interior discussion with herself aloud. "It's no longer just about us."

The man was about to take another sip of his drink, but placed it back on its coaster. It shone golden in the light of a nearby table lamp.

"In case you haven't noticed, we're real, you and I. We have a past together. You can't just ignore it."

"Nobody's trying to ignore it. I just don't want anybody hurt. I don't want anyone's lives broken like, like—"

"You mean like ours were?"

"That was ages ago."

"That's what I mean. People adjust, you know. You can't just ignore reality."

The woman put her drink down on the table harder than she had meant to. "Don't you talk to me about reality, you and your dreams."

The man looked around to see if they had attracted any attention. When he was relatively certain that they hadn't, he spoke in an altogether softer tone. "I can't help it. It's the only happiness I've ever had, being with you."

"Sometimes," the woman began, "sometimes it's selfish to be happy."

She could no longer conceal that she was crying. She opened her purse, presumably looking for some Kleenex. The man pulled his silver pocket handkerchief from his breast pocket and handed it to her. She blew her nose audibly into it, doubling it over upon itself, continued to hold it in front of her face. She was saying something, but the words were indistinguishable.

"I can't hear a damn thing you're saying, by the way," the man said.

She lowered the handkerchief and folded it once more. "I said, we both married other people."

"But we wouldn't have. If your parents hadn't taken you out of town and kept us apart you never would have married Michael, and I—"

"Let's not rerun ancient history."

"Let's do. You seem to have forgotten most of it. I couldn't get a hold of you. They wouldn't let me know where you were. They whisked you out of town—"

"I was so lonely that summer. I kept waiting for you, but you never called."

"I had no way of knowing where they had taken you. Your father kept threatening me."

"What did you expect? We made a mistake, you and I—"

"Mistake? Is that what you call what happened?"

She clutched his silver handkerchief between her fingers and waved it slightly as she spoke. "That's what everybody *else* called it. Yes, it was a mistake. I was too young, too young, is all. So were you."

The man looked down at his cocktail glass. "We're not young anymore."

"No," the woman said, "not anymore."

The waiter appeared and asked them if they would care for an appetizer.

The man said, "No. I mean, we haven't seen a menu."

"I'll get you one, sir." the waiter said. "Ma'am?"

"I'll have another vodka."

"And cranberry?"

"No," she said. "Just the vodka."

"On the rocks?"

"Yes, please."

The woman stirred a swizzle stick in her empty glass. "There's a point where the cranberry juice becomes beside the point." Glancing up she found the man watching her. She looked away. "There's a point where *everything* becomes beside the point."

The waiter reappeared with menus and a fresh drink. "Sir. Ma'am."

When he had gone, the woman said, "He does look like that actor in *La Bamba*. He's sweet. They all are at that age. But I hate when they call me *Ma'am*. It makes me feel so damned old."

The windowpanes of the John Hancock Center shone orange, reflecting the waning sun. A pianist had begun to play cocktail music on the far side of the lounge, and the room began to fill with a fresh wave of patrons in business attire.

The man leaned in close to the woman and said, "She would be just about seventeen now. Has she ever—"

"No."

"You didn't let me finish."

The woman lifted her glass, closed her eyes as she sipped her drink. "But I know what you were going to say. You were going to ask me if she ever tried to get in touch with me, and she hasn't. I hope to God she never does."

"Why do you say that?"

"Because it's ancient history, I told you. A mistake. We have our own lives now, our own families."

"What do you think *we* would have been?"

The woman went to put her glass down on the coffee table and some of the drink spilled over the edge. "Not a family. Don't say it ever would have been a family. It was a shame and a regret—that's what it was, and I hate it. And I hate *you* for reminding me." She held a cocktail napkin to her eyes and turned her back to the man. "What did I do with your damned handkerchief?"

The man picked the handkerchief from the floor where it had fallen and handed it back to her.

"You don't hate *it*," he said. "You hate what they *did* to you— your own parents. The way they made you feel."

"I hate what it would do to your wife and my husband, and our *chil*dren, if they ever found out. That Beemis man—if he saw us, and told his wife, and if she told someone who told *your* wife, think of how she'd feel. Think of what might happen."

"That's about all I've been *able* to think about. Don't you know that? But there comes a time we have to be honest. There comes a time when we have to be honest with *ourselves*."

"Fine. Be honest with yourself. I don't want to talk about it anymore. You promised that this time you wouldn't. You promised."

"All right," the man said.

"You always say you won't, but then you do."

The woman dabbed her eyes with the handkerchief. The man looked down at the carpet, at the tips of his own shoes. "I'm sorry," he said. "I'm sorry for everything."

Slowly, unsteadily at first, the woman stood. "It was such a lovely day," she said. "Such a lovely autumn day." Then she picked up her jacket, her purse, said, "Excuse me," and walked across the lobby to the ladies room.

The man sat back in his chair, gazed abstractedly at the menu— *Foie Gras Torchon, Charcuterie Plate, Venison Pate.* Out the windows the sun's glow had matured to bronze, illuminating the huge lozenge-shaped steel girders of The Hancock Center. A young attractive, well-dressed couple walked by, as though they might have been two mannequins from Nordstrom's come to life. He thought of the blue water of the painting, how it seamlessly met the sky, how inviting it was, with the promise of refreshing coolness and a new beginning.

It was a moment before he realized the waiter was standing beside him.

"Sir? The lady sent you this."

He took the little folded paper from the waiter's hand, nodded. Then he slowly unfolded it:

Darling,

I've taken a cab to the station. Thank you for the
lunch and the afternoon. Please don't disclose my
whereabouts to anyone who might inquire about them
in the near future. You know who I mean. Be happy
with the life you have now. (I still don't believe you
about the lions.)

Love,
Amanda

He let the note fall from his fingertips to the coffee table, and when he looked up it was as if a projector had whirred back into action and he had returned to the world of the present. He checked his watch, calculated that she would easily make the six-eighteen, would return to Portage, to her husband and daughter, the tall girl who rode horses. He remembered waiting outside of her parents' home in an old red Oldsmobile convertible that summer night, so many years ago, till the air grew chill and his back began to ache from fatigue. No one came and no one went. He had finally driven off as the sun rose, a lump of defeat in his throat, her second-story bedroom window growing tinier and tinier in the rearview mirror, until it was out of sight.

Come Summer

Long ago everything seemed right with the world, and I could go about my life in relative peace and quietude, anonymous, at one with the beach, the sidewalks and paths of the town that had grown so dear to me. Every summer of my youth, my family vacationed at our second home in Lake Geneva, Wisconsin, which is where I discovered many things—the art of swimming, the secrets that my teenage sister Lorna kept so darkly hidden, the treasures buried in the local library stacks on lazy afternoons, and a rare and surprising first glimpse into my own heart.

Our backyard sagged slowly to the water's west shore, and on the perimeter of the property a stone path led shaky-kneed visitors to our dock. I sat there, legs dangling above the dark green algae, which danced in slow motion, half-listening to the sounds of bathers on the beach, a constant murmur, not so very much unlike the incessant screech of insects at night. Human insects. Sunlight twinkled on the lake as I pressed the heel of my palm onto the grooves of the aluminum dock walkway, leaving red impressions on my hand. This was 1961—the year Father had unexpectedly sold the boat, without so much as consulting with or announcing his decision to anyone. All that was left were a few white, round lifesavers and limp mooring ropes. At times a child's voice, either laughing or imploring, floated above the water like a disembodied spirit, and I wondered who all those people were, and if they were the same ones every day, or if they went home and others took their place.

I would be twelve soon; I had my own bedroom and attendant responsibilities. I don't recall anyone ever checking up on me, or intruding. I'm not sure if it was a system of trust or just the good luck of benign neglect. Whichever was the case, my room was my glory.

The windows were framed by navy blue curtains featuring World War II fighters engaged in aerial combat—P 51 Mustangs, British Spitfires, German Messerschmitt 109s. On my work table in the far corner was a nearly completed Stuka dive bomber, missing only its wing flaps and canopy. You did not want to rush the building of a good model. You took it in stride, to avoid the smears of glue that might otherwise ruin an inspired effort. On the end table was my record player, top open, a pancake stack of black 45 rpm records ready to play the anthems of the season—"Hello Mary Lou," "Runaway," "Quarter to Three." I'd nearly worn them out. My nightstand was ill-kempt, laden with Superman comic books and a fresh haul of books from the Lake Geneva Public Library: *The Human Comedy*, *Of Mice and Men*, and *The Wonderful Flight to the Mushroom Planet*. I would begin the first of these tomorrow, unaware of the pangs that wartime had in store for me, or the joys that would sustain and redeem Saroyan's Macauley family.

Outside the French windows of the dining room fireflies danced in the warm blanket of night, and the lights from town glimmered faintly upon the lake's surface. I heard my sister Lorna saying something to my mother, upstairs in the hallway, her voice despondent, like the cry of a young calf. Lorna was a college girl now, attended Marquette University in Milwaukee. I lowered the sound of the new television, the better to hear. Lorna asked Mother if she wouldn't please, *please* give the telephone line a rest, said that her young man was supposed to call tonight.

Lorna had a young man, Wallace, and he would be visiting us, if you could believe recent rumors. It was all very occult, Lorna and her young man, the rituals involving sororities, pins and being pinned. He was from a "good" family I had heard, and though I was young, I had no illusions as to what that word really meant. It had nothing to do with virtue, or practicing spontaneous acts of charity. Mother had come downstairs only twice today, both times to refill the ice bucket. Other than that, she spoke tirelessly on the phone, her voice a muffled drone behind a closed door. *Wallace.* His first name sounded like a last name. *Might as well call himself Smith*, I thought.

Maggie was our maid and our cook and she came four days a week. A thin, young black woman, her eyes alternately slashed out at you and receded into weariness. She wore a white uniform and a red-and-white checked scarf around her neck, which at times she pulled up and tightened to keep her hair in place. She called me *Young Sir*. "Have you cleaned your bedroom, Young Sir?"

"Yes, Maggie."

"That your laundry?"

I had an armful of dirty clothes. "Yes, Maggie."

"You make sure you take it to the hamper in the basement, make Maggie's life a little easier."

I had been on my way to the basement anyway, but to this I just nodded. Maggie did not mean to nag; she was just organized, and determined to keep her place. The cool, dank smell of the basement reminded me of the times Father and I had come back from outings with a catch, and we cleaned the fish right near the wash tub, cutting, filleting. That had been some time ago, and now we no longer had the boat. I thought that it would be nice if we could fish together again, perhaps this summer from the dock, though that would not be the same as enjoying the freedom of riding the crests that chopped upon the surface of the lake.

The soft, warm glimpses of those summers come to me as pieces of a dream that have inadvertently fallen from my fingertips. Maggie had made me a bowl of puffed rice, which I ate in front of the new color television, experimenting with the tint control knobs. The gauze curtains of the French windows rode a light breeze as from the kitchen Lorna's wistful voice blended with the solider buzz of outboard motors.

"How did you know with your man, Maggie? That he was the one, I mean."

President Kennedy appeared on TV as Maggie let go a long trail of lilting laughter, as though it had been pent up inside her for too long. The President did not smile, and the First Lady was not at his side. Instead there were troubled looking men in suits gathered around him, hands behind their backs. The announcer said something about national security.

29

Maggie said, "Girl, I couldn't help myself. That man put a *spell* on me."

Their combined laughter spilled from the kitchen, high, and arced like water from a lawn sprinkler, and the curtains furled and unfurled and now I saw that it was true. There was nothing wrong with the color knobs. President Kennedy's hair wasn't black, as it was in the newspapers. It was *red*.

"I think that's how it is with Wallace, too," Lorna said. "I think he put a spell on me."

Then they shrieked in unison again, and there was trouble at the White House, you could plainly see, but I couldn't fathom what it was.

In the misty distance sails billowed upon the lake, ten, twenty of them at a time, slow moving, almost at a standstill, confined to the southern shore where they remained safely isolated from the swollen, rippled wakes of speedboats. An occasional gull glided overhead, wings outstretched, and the sun ricocheted in piercing blasts off the iron croquet wickets that I stuck into the soft, muddy earth of the backyard. Lorna had asked me to please set the course up, though she could very well have done it herself. I supposed she was going to practice before Wallace arrived so she wouldn't look a fool when they played against one another. Eyes closed, she sunned in just her bathing suit upon a chaise longue at the top of the yard. She even wore Wallace's pin on that, her navy one-piece swim suit, white thighs caressed by golden sunlight. She was a pretty girl, and there was something sad about her being alone, wearing that silly lavaliere. Her small breasts rose and fell as she breathed, and I secretly watched them for a while. I wondered if President Kennedy and Jackie did it—but of course they did. They had children, and so they must have, right inside the White House, with all the guards and cooks and Secret Service men about, a regular crowd. I guess he couldn't help himself. She was, after all, Jackie.

I measured the distance for the next wicket, when suddenly an outboard motor choked and sputtered and wheezed and then roared. It startled me so that I lost my balance there in the pitched yard, almost went rolling down the hill like a log. I could hear Lorna chuckle to herself, a mean trick. I had thought her eyes had been closed all the while I'd been watching her.

In the boat slip next to ours, a young girl around my age adjusted the throttle of a Mercury outboard motor from inside a white Boston Whaler. It was a small boat by any standard, perhaps thirteen feet at most, though very popular with the young people who lived on the lake. You could go pretty well in them, get them up to about twenty-five or thirty knots, though they had squared bows and bounced like there was no tomorrow. I had never seen this girl before, and wondered if she was a guest of the neighbors, or if her parents had recently bought the house. I had lost count of my strides and decided to put the next rung in any old where. The girl wore red shorts with white stripes on the side, and had a slightly upturned nose. Faint freckles sprinkled her cheeks, and she had gotten some sunburn on her arms, though her feet and toes were pale in contrast. She disregarded me as if I were part of the lawn set.

"Go on and introduce yourself, "Lorna called out from the top of the yard.

Everything echoes upon the lake, especially a voice. The girl looked over at me and I turned my back upon her fiercely, glaring at my sister, anxious and willing to do nothing short of disemboweling myself right there on the lawn. I let the extra wickets drop to the ground with a dull clank and suggested to Lorna, "You might as well finish the job yourself, what with being in a *spell* and all."

◆

In the afternoons I would sit in a carrel at a dead end in the stacks of the Lake Genevea Public Library, under rows of white-blue fluorescent tubes. It was cool and dry, a haven from the scorching heat of the beach, though situated right next door to it, and it smelled of aged paper and leather, the leaves and bindings of thousands of accumulated volumes. It was a private, wonderful place, where Homer Macauley reluctantly delivered telegrams to unnerved mothers, and George and Lennie, confined to a dreary bunkroom, dreamed of owning their own little home. Lennie would feed the rabbits.

Afterward I strolled down Broad Street to the cinema, stood gaping at the larger- than-life posters advertising the summertime fright festivals. They had begun to piggy-back current releases with vintage science fiction films—the former to bring in the staid adult crowd, the latter to cater to the town's considerable teenage tourist population. *Kronos, The Blob*. In one poster rendition Steve McQueen was featured shielding his date (a sumptuous brunette, limply collapsed in his arms) from a huge purple bubble that had engulfed the local diner and threatened civilization, at least as far as the local supermarket. What would the summer be without seeing *The Blob*?

If I had a dollar in my pocket I'd stop at the drug store soda counter and order a milk shake, or else a chocolate phosphate. At three in the afternoon I had the place to myself, and the soda jerk usually gave me two cherries embedded in a thick, rich top layer of genuine Wisconsin whipped cream. Life could hardly get better than this, though I thought vaguely of the girl at the boat slip, and wondered why my father had not yet driven up to our summer home. What was it that investment bankers did, other than invest, and couldn't they do that over the phone, anyway?

After a particularly splendid shake (three cherries), I arrived home one late afternoon to find my mother entertaining Lillian, a friend of hers. Next to the coffee table in the living room lay several shopping bags from the local dress emporium, where only the wealthy local residents shopped. Lillian owned a home half a mile down the road, a huge Victorian built upon a bluff that had once belonged to a famous Chicago industrialist. From her back yard you could see the Yerkes Observatory over in Williams Bay, home to the world's largest refracting telescope. Lillian had bleached hair and smelled dimly reminiscent of mothballs.

"Where have you been?" Mother asked, talking to me as she bent over the roll-away bar, pouring a drink for her company. Her eyes were red-rimmed and she seemed hazy, preoccupied.

I said I had gone to the library, and then I asked her when Father would be coming. At this she stopped pouring from the decanter, held it suspended above the glass as if posing for a photograph.

"We'll talk about that later. Go clean your room."

Lillian shaped the ash of her cigarette in a green, glass ashtray on the end table. Swirls of gray smoke rose, suspended by serried rows of afternoon sunlight filtered through the Venetian blinds.

"Can I see *The Blob*?" I asked.

"Certainly not," Mother said, handing off the drink distractedly to Lillian. "It might upset you."

"But—"

"See to your room, please."

She would not look at me as she spoke, and I noticed a tremor in her hand, a slight slur in her speech. This was not her first drink today. She had a high forehead, my mother did, and sandy brown hair arranged in a semi-bouffant. Most women were coiffed that way back then, but on my mother that style looked particularly authentic. She possessed an aristocratic air that she could neither disguise nor fully conceal at any time that I was ever aware of. It was part of who she was, but I always had the impression that she was not wholly comfortable with it.

As Lillian sipped her aperitif she looked at me over the edge of her glass with big, bovine eyes, as if I were a local curiosity. Lillian didn't have any children. She had money instead.

A formless, indefinite feeling of unease had settled over the house, the lake, my own being, an inimical heft. Whether it was because of Father's absence, Mother's voluntary seclusion, Lorna's pining for her young man, or a combination of all these things, I couldn't say, but it was there, and it was real and there was nothing I could do about it. One nightfall I strode down the stone steps of the backyard under a starry sky, alone near the shore, as a large, slow moving sightseeing boat floated by, spilling yellow light into the dark from a flared bank of windows. The hum of adult voices was punctuated by the clink of cocktail glasses and soon the silhouetted craft grew small and silence settled once more upon the water. At that instant a light winked on in the house next door and I saw the girl from the boat slip. She had her back to me and seemed to be arranging something on top of a bureau. There were hedges separating our properties, and I moved closer to them, clung to their branches to obscure myself, and continued watching her as I held my breath out of fear I might make a sound, somehow alert her. A mirror on a far wall allowed me to see her face—the slightly turned-up nose, which I happily remembered, bangs cut oval-shaped above her forehead. Her eyes were large and set far apart, and her small, shapely ears seemed designed to hold her straight, swept-back hair in place. At least, this was the use to which she put them. There was just the girl, the night, and I—along with perhaps ten thousand or so crickets keeping secret my presence. I could not, *dared* not move, suspended as I was between fear and something very different from fear. All at once she drew up her t-shirt and whisked it over her head. The pink skin of her neck flowed seamlessly into broad shoulders, pale nipples, torso tapering to the narrowest of waists. My legs gave as if having been pulled out from under me, and I fell hard upon the stone pathway. Hurt and alarmed, worried that I'd given myself away, I scrambled back up the hill to our house. Looking back, I saw only the lights from the opposite shore shimmering conspiratorially upon the darkened lake.

The leaves of the trees were sun-faded and drooped in the morning heat, another scorcher on the way. I chucked my way past the bed and breakfasts of North Street, their freshly painted wooden signs hanging from polished brass hinges above clumps of crabgrass. They looked so neat and clean; the tourists must have thought so too, for there were no vacancies. I had planned to visit the old observatory for some time, only now in late July finally getting around to it. The sole means of travel to Williams Bay, for a boy my age, anyway, was to hitchhike, the hills in that direction being prohibitive, too steep to ride by bike, more than a full day's walk. I followed Route 50 west, a good way out of the business district, and failed at my first two attempts—one old farmer in a rickety pick-up paid no heed, and next a postal worker wagged an accusatory finger at me as his truck shushed past, stirring the morning heat. I thought at once of my new secret—the girl from the dock in her nakedness, and now the memory of her, furtive, unrepentant, played upon my mind, and I held it close, a gift. I knew I should have been ashamed of myself, but I wasn't.

A sudden crunch of gravel shot from the road's surface, sent a roiling cloud of clay-colored dust into the air. A beaten, red convertible skitched to a halt at my side, whisking me back from the shrubs outside the girl's bedroom last night under a sprinkle of stars, beside the faint echo of lights cast upon the lake. I hadn't even seen it approaching, the car, having come virtually out of nowhere, leaving me shaken and short of breath. A fine grit settled slowly upon the hood, the wild weeds at the roadside, my sneakers. The driver was a middle-aged man with a day or two's growth of beard upon a weathered and creased face, the opaque green lenses of his sunglasses concealing his eyes, perhaps a deal more, rendering him aloof. He drew hard upon a cigarette that had already burned down to the filter tip, then snapped it away into the brittle brush of the roadside with a flourish. The passenger door of the car opened, or else I opened it, I can no longer say for sure which, and I stood gazing at the interior, at the leather boot of the stick shift, the worn, wooden dashboard with all the esoteric dials and gauges, the faded black steering wheel with chrome spokes.

Not another car traveled in either direction as far as I could see. The silence upon the road was unnatural, the sun hotter and more demanding than usual. "Get in," he said, without looking at me, staring off straight ahead with dead resolve, disconnected from the rest of the world by the twin walls of his Ray-Ban shades. He spoke to me as if he were a neighbor, or someone who'd been at the house, as if we'd been introduced and I had clean forgotten who he was. The air was dry and thick. I wiped my sweating brow with my forearm, and before I even realized I had gotten in, the car shot off down the deserted highway with a dull roar that I could feel throbbing within my throat.

Outside, trees and farm fields swooshed by in a frenetic rush, but inside all was still, like the eye of a localized hurricane. It occurred to me in a moment of steel-cold understanding that he had not asked me where I was headed. I cupped my hand protectively on the door lever.

"I'm going to Yerkes Observatory," I announced in general, with the effect of having declared my rank and serial number.

The man neither altered his expression nor responded. His hand, sheathed in a torn leather driving glove, palmed the gearshift, opened

35

around it, clasped it again, jerking it in quick, measured movements. He drove fast, faster than any adult I had ever driven with, his steering harsh and quirky, like that of a race car driver's. He veered left over the oncoming lane and off-roaded it, nicking the delta of a grass-covered island. In a flush of hot panic I wondered if I had, at the age of eleven, already made the fatal mistake that my parents had so often warned against at odd moments just before bedtime, or as I left home for the bus stop.

"You oughtn't to waste a day such as this in a place such as that. Plenty of other adventures for a boy to be seeing to, before it's all over."

This struck me as an ominous piece of advice.

"How's that?"

For the first time his expression changed; he smiled a smirky smile, reminded me of an eagle. He produced another cigarette from a monogrammed shirt pocket—an iridescent green, the shirt, the color of a June insect—and coolly lit it by scraping a wooden match against the rugged fabric of his dungarees. "Summer's nearly over. For a boy, when summer's gone—so is everything, just about. Isn't that right?"

Dust blew from the hood and cicadas droned from hidden places. "I guess so."

"Locked up in a museum on a summer afternoon. That's all it is, the observatory, a museum. Not what it's cracked up to be." He tilted his head in self-agreement and exhaled a long trail of cigarette smoke. "You take Yerkes. You'd figure a man who built an observatory would've had a deep and abiding interest in astronomy and the universe and the like, wouldn't you?"

I had no idea who Yerkes had been. "Sure," I said.

"Not old Yerkes," he said, spitting out the driver's side. "He never so much as looked up at the sky to make sure it was still there. Got himself in a jam with the law—transportation scandal. When he fronted the money for that telescope, he was just trying to reclaim his reputation." He turned to me with a wide-mouthed grin. "Wanted to hang out with the big-shot socialites again. Yerkes didn't know asteroids from Shinola. Rainey Harper was the guy who bled him dry, President of the University of Chicago. Respectable fellow, you'd say. College man—hm? Had Yerkes pay for the telescope—and then tricked him into funding the whole building, kept telling him he'd become accepted by the hoity-toity, which was all he ever wanted, anyway. Held what you'd call *seemliness* in front of him like some kind of caste carrot, and he fell for it, the poor sap." He laughed here, and I wondered if he were a professor, or some kind of ruined astronomer.

We had begun the winding assent to Williams Bay. His right hand alternately steadied the steering wheel and worked the gearshift, the motor sighing in response. I had not yet had to worry about losing seemliness. Social chicanery escaped me. "What do you mean?" I said.

He ejected a burned-out stub into the wind and popped yet another fresh cigarette into the side of his mouth, his short sandy hair alive in the breeze. "Kid—get wise. It was a rip-off. Harper didn't give a damn about Yerkes or his social standing, which, by the way, he never *did* get back. And Yerkes didn't care about the solar system. You could've knocked him over the head with Pluto and he wouldn't've known the difference. But here you are, all these years later, on your way to a great and venerable institution with a big telescope—the biggest, mind you—named after a jailbird, who was bilked by an opportunist, while what's left of the summer is dying all around you." Hands cupped around the cigarette, he scratched another match—driving no-handedly, making my heart skip a beat as we careened toward an oncoming lawn maintenance truck. At the last second he nudged the steering wheel, righted our course. "Nothing's quite what it seems," he said, addressing me via the windshield. "Is it?"

He smiled at me obliquely, blew out a geyser of blue-gray smoke. Dappled sunlight found its way through overhanging boughs and raced upon the faded finish of the car's hood. The steady rush of fresh air lulled me, and for a moment I had forgotten where we were going, the summer afternoon sprawling lazily in every direction. There was a disturbing truth in what he said. The fields were duller than they had been earlier in the summer, the leaves of trees insect-eaten. The very breeze itself carried upon it the notice of the season's demise, and suddenly the July day altered, became nothing so much as an early preview of autumn. At last we pulled into the observatory's long drive, curled around the cul-de-sac, and I let myself out. The stranger looked older now than I had estimated as he trained his thick, dark lenses on me, his mechanical grin glistening as if he'd tripped some kind of switch. And in the shade of the Yerkes' gardens the fantastic car now appeared a faint blue rather than red. The big dome of the telescope towered above, cathedral-like, blotting out a good portion of the sky. I turned and walked up the shadowed marble steps.

"Have you learned her name?" That is exactly what I thought I'd heard him say.

I spun around and found him grinning equivocally. "Pardon?" I asked.

He took the cigarette from his mouth and lowered his head, as though addressing the curbside. "I said, '*You've earned your day.*'"

The motor revved, exhaust rumbled, and he sped off down the drive, shifting once, twice, the grunt of gears disappearing into the relative silence of the lonely Wisconsin afternoon. Sunshine flickered on his chrome bumper momentarily like a flap of celluloid at the end of a movie reel. I stood alone on the stone steps, wondering what he meant, and exactly what had just occurred.

The gray Volkswagen was parked on our inclined drive like a bug caught in something sticky. I knew it belonged to Wallace, and I knew I would be forced to shake hands with him, even as the woman who had given me the ride home put the finishing touches to her scolding about the dangers of hitchhiking, a subject upon which I was more expert than she.

"Wallace Eli Steffan," my sister said smugly, as though trumping me in Bridge, "this is my little brother." Wallace extended his brawny hand, replete with amethyst class ring, barely taking me in, eyes trained esuriently on something just above my head. He was about six-one or six-two (six-two if you counted the flattop), and he wore black chinos, white socks, and black, penniless loafers. He could have been a stand-in on a Kingston Trio album cover, or any of a million or so other college men back in 1961. My aversion to him was instinctive and instantaneous. There was about him a rather constant effusion of innocent denial.

When I turned around to see what he had been staring at, I caught, through the freshly cleaned French windows, a brief glimpse of my girl at the dock in a two-piece turquoise swimsuit, bending somewhat to fasten the mooring rope to her Whaler. When Wallace's eyes finally found my line of vision, and it took some time for that to happen, he looked as though he had just taken the Boy Scout pledge. I think I can trace my first murderous impulse to that precise moment.

My mother made a rare and rather startling appearance, clinging to the banister of the staircase, tripping somewhat as she reached the landing. When she greeted Lorna's young man by name, she gave it an extra syllable ("Wa-uh-lace") and it should have been clear to everyone that she was plastered out of her skull. I had never seen her quite like that before, and couldn't fathom why she had done it to herself. There would be no escape from the table that night, where I was forced to endure the longest and most abysmal dinner of my young life. I thought of the stranger, wondered what his take on Wallace would have been, but of course I already knew. He would have sized him up in a moment, cut through his phony veneer with a cold and blank appraising stare. I let my fork rearrange the mashed potatoes on my plate, learned that Wallace played rugby and was the vice president of his fraternity. *Sigma Alpha Fraud*, I thought.

The stranger had been right about the observatory as well. There were no great astronomical discoveries going on inside. In fact, there was just one man in the entire place, a bald-headed fellow with a bow tie who only had time to show me a few photos of the moon.

"You are looking at the Sea of Tranquility," he said.

"All right," I said.

His mealy voice echoed in the stark corridors. "Here is a small mountainous region. Can you see it?"

"Yes." It looked dead.

There was abrupt laughter at the table over something Wallace had said. My mother spilled her water and I wished she would just go back up to her room, the evening having already become painful enough.

Maggie had stayed late to make dinner, and by offering to help her clear the table I won a sort of quasi-reprieve. Plates stacked one on top of the other, I shouldered the swinging kitchen door and Maggie followed with a silver platter full of crystal glasses. "I'm afraid your mother's not feeling well tonight," she said.

"She's shit-faced, Maggie."

I can still see her in a frozen moment of bewilderment, ready to either admonish me about my language or perhaps burst out laughing. The kitchen door shoved open brusquely and there was Wallace, all of him. He strode over to Maggie, he and his flattop and his square shoulders, and held out a set of car keys. "My bags are in the trunk of my car," he said, in a tone as dispassionate as the glaze in his eyes.

He might as well have struck her. Her face transformed as though it had absorbed the force of his words and the passive brutality that lingered behind them.

Wallace twirled the keychain around his finger several times, the tensed musculature of his arms rippling against the sleeves of his broadcloth oxford shirt, his eyes never veering from hers. At last Maggie's hand slowly lifted and clasped the keys. His lips stretched in a taut smile of recognition, and he turned and left the room. A faint trace of Aqua Velva lingered in the close air of the kitchen.

"You stay here, Maggie," I said. "*I'll* go get his bags."

When she put her arms around me from behind, I could feel the pumping of her pulse within her veins. "You watch out for him, child," Maggie warned me in a parched whisper. "He's trouble. He's *real* trouble."

He had hurt her in a way I had never known a person could be hurt before, and though my hatred for him was almost aberrant, I understood what I was up against, sensed just what an advantage he held.

The sun was nothing more than a blear purple at the horizon, the water lapping lazily at the shore, a lover begging for favors. I stood under the sanctum of the girl's window with a handful of pebbles and not quite enough determination to launch them. *If Father were here*, I thought, *if only Father were here.* So many things had changed that summer, and I had changed with them. The world, once a pretty comfortable place, now felt cold and foreign, and perhaps because I was so bitterly alone in it, I randomly let fly a volley of tiny rocks against the windowpane with such force that I was at first afraid that I had shattered it. It took almost no time at all for her to appear, the light from her bedroom lamp forming a corona around her. She struggled with the window lock as she shimmied the old wooden frame up.

"What do you want?" she demanded.

"Do you want to see *The Blob*?"

"What?" she asked. "Are you crazy?"

"It's a movie playing at the cinema. Do you want to go see it with me?"

The night was abuzz with the susurration of insects and the predatory roar of car mufflers halted at intersections. We cut a direct path to the theater through the night, neon blinking around us in 1960's pastels of pink and green, and oh, the loveliness of that young face beneath the string-straight hair, the pushed-up nose, those young chapped lips. I had ravaged my mother's purse secretly for the ticket fare, something I'd never done before, something for which to this day I am secretly disgraced. But I was broke and the moment would not wait, would never present itself again, and Mother would never know anyway, because to her it was just pocket change, and because, well, because she was the way she was.

"What is the Blob?" the girl asked me.

"It's this thing," I said. "No one really knows what it is, but it's this thing, and it isn't good." That's what I had surmised up to that point.

She sat beside me in the darkened theater, her bare leg inches from mine, stretching out of Levi's shorts rolled once or twice above knee-level, her white skin visible in the bluish haze of the projector's light. If I could have reached out and touched it, if only. A couple in front of us by three rows was necking so animatedly that they upstaged McQueen for the first ten minutes of the feature, but then there was the meteor, the old man with the glop on his hand, and McQueen looking so perfect, so familiar, somehow. He alone recognized the danger of the Blob; everyone else in the town seemed to be sleepwalkers, oblivious. He ran, he protested, he shouted, and all the while I kept thinking, *He's not a teenager. He's old.* The Blob itself was a preposterous purple bubble, about as frightening as a bowl of Jell-O. What was ghastly, absolutely petrifying, was the somnolence of the town's population, their failure to sense their own vulnerability. I looked at the girl beside me. She was absorbed in the thirty-five millimeter series of prints spinning on the screen. For her, the whole of existence lay there. For me, the world and all its contents were encapsulated within her. I could not get enough, could not take my eyes off of her.

The answer was so simple. Co_2. You kill a Blob with stuff that was nothing more than the mere exhalation of a breath.

"Were you frightened?" the girl asked me, on our walk home. The uneven patches of sidewalk sparkled like diamond dust in the midnight glow of streetlights.

"No.

"I'll bet you were."

"Just by how stupid the people were."

When we reached her jarred window she turned to me and asked with almost formal earnestness, "You wanna go on a ride in my boat sometime?"

The blue sheen of lake-reflected light tinted her cheek. I simply nodded.

"We'll have to do it early in the morning so my parents don't know. I'll knock on your window."

I wanted to lower my head and kiss those summer-dried lips, but she hopped up upon a garden stone and squirmed and lifted herself through her open window, leaving me alone in the insect-loud night. Or so I had first thought. As I walked up the pathway to our house I heard sounds coming from the back porch. I crouched there in the yard by the old birch tree, listening to soft moans in the night. I hid from a shaft of piercing moon glow down by the shrubbery and the porch's lattice work.

"Did you hear something?"

Lorna's whisper was unmistakable. I crept closer, listened for a response, but there was none, just a fullish gasp, a sigh, another gasp. Perched upon my knees I drew the courage to peek through the screened window. At first I did not understand what I was seeing, that in the murky shadows they had become one. Lorna's dress lay discarded in a heap upon the floor, the lavaliere bathed in lush, silver light. It was an aching, dull discovery, and it honed my hatred for Wallace to needle-like sharpness. The water rolled upon the shore, prompting the slithery sound of pebbles sliding into relentless waves. There was the smell of rain in the air.

"Where have you been?"

Mother had caught me sneaking in the front door. She seemed more herself now, though she looked utterly terrible, her face lined and haggard in the yellow lamplight, as though she hadn't slept in a week. How I wished that she could be young and pretty as she had been at the beginning of the season before everything had happened, wished that Father had been with us, that things could be just the way they used to be. I thought of the moon, that desolate place, that lonely, desolate place.

"The porch," I said.

"What?"

"Just go out to the back porch, Mother."

◆

The unexpected knock upon my window came at dawn on the very day we were to return home from the lake. I climbed into my Levi's that had been lying on the floor next to the bed, parted the curtains, the Messerschmitts from the Mustangs, and beheld her face in the pink moment before sunrise. She had said she would come to get me, and now she was here, after weeks of patient waiting, followed by the stillborn certainty of disappointment. I slid the window up and crawled noiselessly out of the house. Not a word was spoken. We raced to the lake like the wind, happy and free, our time at last. The girl, my girl, handily untied the knots of the mooring ropes and shoved hard against the dock piling, sending us floating upon the buoyant waves. When we had drifted a good way out, our houses many times smaller than they had been, she let rip the cord of the Mercury engine and it clamored in response. Soon the hull lifted, the water pounded hard beneath us, and we skittered ever closer to a destination that had been charted for us not so much by ourselves as by nature.

I hadn't had to think twice about it, triggering Wallace's midnight and permanent banishment, though I hadn't counted on Lorna's heartbreak, for which I felt genuinely sorry. He'd never called again, and for weeks my poor sister had been inconsolable, a recluse in self-imposed exile, confined to the dreary gloom of her shuttered bedroom. At times when I felt most strongly the sting of remorse, I'd bring her lemonade or iced tea, but she'd never have any. "She's got the achies, Young Sir," Maggie would tell me, as I returned the glass to the kitchen sink. "But better small ones now than big ones later."

I thought so, too.

The girl shut down the engine, letting the boat drift aimlessly in the fresh new morning. We lay curled up on the deck against one another. The summer strayed effortlessly away as I held her, transparent images playing upon my mind like cottontail dust in the breeze. When Mother had sat me down to ask me if I understood what divorce would mean, I simply nodded. Father hadn't been living with us anyway, and so the matter seemed less profound than her expression seemed to suggest.

"Things are different now," my girl said.

"I know," I said.

"Ever since the stranger."

The stranger. So she knew about him, too.

"Shh," I said. "Let's don't talk about him."

Sunlight sparkled randomly upon her eyelashes, amber, orange and pearl, tiny kaleidoscopes. Gulls cried, a plaintive sound. Through all these trifling wonders the boat continued to rock back and forth upon the water.

"Will you come next year?" she asked.

"Yes."

"Then I'll wait for you."

◆

After packing my suitcase I sat in the car behind my sister, waiting for Mother to finish locking up. Lorna's dejection had matured into a sullen anger, which she wore in the form of a fixed and subtle frown. The radio played "Runaround Sue," and I remember that Dion sounded lonely without the Belmonts, the voices of a nameless choir embellishing his own. Chevys lost their fins that year, and Allan Shepard was a hero after having been sealed in a capsule and hurtled into icy space. Father would move to his own apartment. I sat pondering the interminable length of a year, yearning for the fresh mysteries and a return to the familiar world that lay ahead—the bathers and their murmuring sound, the expanse of the July sky, the rich, bracing scent of the lake.

Lorna abruptly snapped off the radio and began sobbing softly. Her hands read like a diary—chipped polish on bitten fingernail stubs. A light rain began to fall, transparent droplets daubing the windshield.

"Don't cry, Lorna," I said.

She sniffed a few times, then gurgled, "I don't want to go."

"It's nothing," I said, brushing away the hand I'd had in her fate as though it were a pestering fly. "Things will be better. Everything will be the same as it was, come summer. You'll see."

She turned upon me ferociously, the hard steel of her voice catching me by surprise. "No it won't be the same. Nothing will. They're selling the house, you little idiot. Don't you know that? Don't you know *anything*?"

And like that it is gone, all of it—my dreams of summers to be, the place of my childhood—evaporated. Like the breath of an intimate friend it is near me and disappears. I think of the girl from the boat slip, of our early morning abandonment. I never even knew her name.

Connecticut Holiday

Marder, fresh from his morning shave, mind still in neutral, sipped tepid coffee and glanced out the living room window at the pocket of pedestrians waiting zombie-like in the cruddy slush to cross Seventh Avenue. He did not hear the portable TV in the kitchen playing the whistled theme of *The Andy Griffith Show,* did not see Opie stoop to pick up the stone, throw it, and rejoin his father on the dirt road in their time-frozen world of perpetual syndication. On the small glass table beside him lay twenty or so student essays, recently graded, covered in red as though hemorrhaging. Marder was thinking about how much he did not want to attend his ex-wife's Christmas dinner, even though his daughters, the beloved little girls who'd had the audacity to grow up behind his back and who rarely called anymore unless they needed three hundred dollars, in a hurry ("Thank you, Daddy!") would be there. A sharp pain stabbed the right side of his gut as he pictured the luxurious house in Litchfield, the one Camille's new husband had bought her five years ago as a wedding present. Howard. Howard the showy bastard. Howard the showy, wife-stealing bastard. That had been just six months after Camille surprised Marder, made good on an old threat and walked out on and divorced him, setting a New York litigational speed record in the process.

Natural for the girls to go off on their own, make their way in the world. Ophelia, the oldest, now a pre-law graduate of DePaul University, had inherited her mother's confidence and organizational abilities, along with her mother's sleek jawbone, and cute butt. Tess, the youngest, hadn't inherited anything from either of them. A freshman at Arizona State, she gathered barely passing grades and bohemian boyfriends who dressed in black and hadn't smiled since Phish played their farewell concert. Marder knew damned well that if he stayed away, he might be spared the painful humiliation of having rejection and failure rubbed in his face, but stapled to this considerable benefit came the inevitable outcome that he would not see the girls again till spring, if then.

The light changed and the pedestrians crossed, and the unexpected memory of carrying Tess home on his shoulders when he had been a big-shot vice president at Foote, Cone and Belding and she only seven, right there on that same slushy corner, ambushed him, lingered. Size three Reeboks on his shoulder. Daddy's girl. He swallowed his longing away with bitter coffee. What could you do about it, anyway? He was late to class.

"Howard? If you're going to take the eight-forty-seven into town you have exactly three minutes to eat your breakfast. If that." Camille set down half a pink grapefruit on the place setting next to a bowl of dry oat bran and a cup of fat-free decaffeinated café au lait. She paused a moment, studying a slightly chipped, French lacquered fingernail, and removed a stray string from the pants of the black suit she found for only $179 in clearance at Neiman Marcus just two weeks earlier, the downtown store, not the one at the mall.

"I haven't got time for breakfast," Howard announced, fitting a well-toned bicep into the sleeve of his suit coat. He lifted and sipped the cup of café au lait and missed the little twitch of irritation at the corner of Camille's mouth.

"You could at least eat some of the grapefruit. Someone I know spent some time slicing all the little whatchamacallits for you."

Howard set his cup back in its saucer, pursed his lips together as he drank. He stepped in close toward Camille, embraced her with some force, one arm around her slender waist, and said, "Someone I know is the prettiest girl on the block. I'll make it up to you tonight after dinner." He kissed her hard upon her cheek, leaving a trace of coffee breath while he struggled into his overcoat. The image of Camille's father at the breakfast table when she had been a little girl stole into her thoughts, gave her a twinge of regret, then faded as she remembered the forest green matchbook she'd found, the scribbled name, the phone number.

"Is Gerry-the-loser coming for Christmas dinner?"

Camille's brow wrinkled under her bangs. "Don't call him that," she said. "He's depressed, is all."

"I'd be depressed if I were him too. The sixty-thousand-a-year man."

"He made more when he was still with Foote."

"He's not with Foote anymore. They wised up."

The bowl of oat bran was whisked from the table, flakes tumbling into the trash can under the sink like brown paper confetti. "You're not attractive when you do this, Howard. You've won the war. You can send the artillery home."

Howard lacked what in other men functioned as emotional Doppler, but he didn't need it now to understand that he had once again behaved the boor and hurt his wife, however unintentionally, for it was written all across her back, which she strategically turned to him from her position at the sink. It had been four days since they had made love, sensational love at that (at least he thought *he'd* performed sensationally), and he didn't want to risk ruining the possibilities that lay ahead that night. Nor did he need complications when he would eventually announce his upcoming business trip, the timing of which was so lousy (Christmas!). He brusquely strode the marble tile back to his wife, commandeered her torso in his arms, and kissed her vigorously upon the mouth. "I'm sorry, C-C." C-C was his pet name for her. She had no idea where he'd come up with it. "I didn't mean it."

She touched her tongue to her bruised lip. It hurt for an hour afterward.

◆

Nowhere is Holden Caulfield's homosexual
identity more apparent than the scene in which he
comes to fisticuffs with his dorm mate at Pencey Prep.
'Straddled' by the dominant 'Stradlater' (the name is
no coincidence; he has mounted Holden and remains

in the superior upright position while Holden is submissively supine), 'Holden' 'holds out,' or attempts to, by displaying a mock-belligerent attitude. **'I was on the goddamn floor and he was sitting on my chest, with his face all red . . . he weighed about a ton. He had hold of my wrists.'** Note particularly the color red, rife with implications of virginal bleeding, our young virgin deflowered, his figurative hymen pierced, as is further stressed in the next passage: **'You never saw such gore in your life. I had blood all over my mouth and chin and even my pajamas. . . '** . Here Holden unwittingly testifies to his brutal, sado-masochistic, para-homo-erotic assault, and what is more, he seems fascinated by it.

Marder tossed the research paper on his desk and tapped a pencil eraser on it thoughtfully as he stared into the face of its young author, Donald Gray, a junior in his American Studies class. Donald sat slumped in a chair beside Marder's cluttered desk, picking nervously at his cuticles. He had seven piercings in the lobe of one ear, which doubled its width—a fact that Marder found remarkable—and his hair was red. And pink. And yellow.

Marder tried to suppress an audible groan, then said, "You don't want to say those things about Holden."

"Yes, I do."

Para-homo-erotic-assault, thought Marder. *God.* "Naw, you don't."

Donald Gray tilted his chin in response. "Oh? And why is that?"

Tap-tap-tap. The pencil eraser. "You want the technical explanation, or the general one?"

"I'd like you to be as specific as you can. Give me the technical one."

"Okay. It's bullshit."

Gray blanched, then reddened. He was more colorful by the

moment. "What about the general one?"

"It's a *lot* of bullshit."

Marder liked his students, he really did. But he'd lost many things in his day—his wife, two daughters, his advertising position and the self-respect that had come with it, two hundred thousand dollars a year, stock options and bonuses, his luxury co-op apartment. He was not about to give up *Catcher*, or *Huck*, or *Moby Dick*, or any of the few genuine pleasures that yet remained for him.

With a sudden outward thrust of his hand, the angry, frightened Gray clutched his paper from Marder's desk, promising, "I'm going to see the dean."

"Okay. Could you ask him for me if we're still on for lunch tomorrow?"

◆

Lyla Hoden called to order the fourteenth meeting of the faculty Copyrights and Patents Committee, an auspicious opportunity, as Marder viewed it, to catch up on his sleep. "Do faculty members perform works for hire when they write lectures for distance learning?" Lyla asked, the sandpaper of her voice scraping against the grain of everyone's sensibilities. "And should the college then be able to market those lectures for profit?" Marder thought, *Will Batman regain consciousness before the speeding train runs off the damaged bridge? And can he untie and save Robin before the Boy Wonder soils his tights?*

He didn't miss meetings with account executives, or the arguments he'd had with the research department over whether certain phrases tested well, the same way he didn't miss the duodenal ulcer he had nursed along. He *did* resent the way it had been done to him, the firing—new regime clean-up of the old guard. Hang anybody who had been associated with the former general. And it had been exciting to open up a random magazine to find his own copy in print ads. But learning to live simply hadn't been insurmountable, as he had lived simply before, when he was young, when he and Camille moved in together. He gazed out beyond the squash-shaped Lyla at the overhead projector's screen and recalled their first Christmas, how he'd bought

Camille the only thing he could afford—a Quicksilver Messenger Service album, the fold-out kind, and later when they listened to it, they rolled fat joints and made love on the hardwood floor next to the orange-crate coffee table in their living room/bedroom, where he discovered for the first time a little row of brown moles along the backside of her thigh, a discovery he ranked right up there with electricity, or penicillin.

But things change. Anyone who has lived has lived more than one life, and that was one of Marder's old ones. The thing to do was to keep plugging away. He had his beloved literature, his work, the car. On some Friday nights, that new little adjunct, what's-her-name, came by to share Chinese, a bottle of wine, a corner of his heart. Sometimes it was almost enough. What was her name? Lana. Lana Almendinger.

◆

Panting, red-faced, Marder just made the first step of the train at 59th Street. It lurched, causing him to jab a hand at the nearest pole to steady himself, and he twisted his elbow in an effort to remain upright. Part of the spoils of war—his balance, limb coordination, muscle tone— that had gone to the victor, time. Off at Queensborough Plaza, he followed the black-gray-tweed overcoated backs of nameless people to the opposite side of the platform where the Flushing Main Street train would pick them up and go and stop and go and stop till he would want to murder the engineer. Above ground now, Marder regarded the fouled snowscape that looked as though every dog in New York had shit upon it.

"Honk the horn twice," Marder instructed, handing a tip to the cabby who'd picked him up at the IRT station.

The cabby frowned, wrinkled his brow. "Huh?"

"Go ahead and honk the horn."

"Orn?" He'd mastered English (a language that reminded him of his homeland's countryside, loaded with hidden land mines) well enough to say *Where you go?* and *Not in my cab, you don't,* but this horn stuff, it sounded weird. He knew the word *horny* and he was about to tell Marder, *"Not in my cab, you don't."*

Marder said, "Honk-honk!" and pointed at the steering wheel.

"Ohhh!" A Checkered epiphany. "Hawnk-hawnk!" the cabby repeated, pounding the padded center of the steering wheel with both hands.

Immediately the door to Pete's Garage rumbled into action, rose jerkily, allowing a view of mechanics with grease-covered arms, up to their elbows, cars on lifts, a silver Mirage, gray Taurus—and in the back, parked on ground level in its own section, a dream. It was beyond sleek and fast. It was beauty in the Keatsian sense, delivered down through the decades to Marder by way of his father's lopsided last will and testament, which had left the eight-million dollar temporary medical help business to his stepmother, and the car to him. But the car—a 1961 Corvette, gold, with white side panels, the first model to incorporate the soon-to-come Stingray sloped backside with recessed taillights, the automotive equivalent of Michelangelo's *Pietà*. It boasted a V-8 engine, Powerglide™ transmission, glass-packed twin mufflers, General Dual-90 tires, and an optional fiberglass hard-top. Marder beheld it as he entered Pete's Garage in Babylon, Long Island. One hundred and fifty a month to house and maintain it. Not a bad deal. Pete drove it to church every Sunday to keep the battery up. To Marder, it was a wasted trip. The car itself was church, its dashboard, an altar.

He fingered the key in his palm, inserted it in the lock. Marder's father had lived in Florida. When he swung open the door, the interior smelled salty, oceanic, like the inside of a boat's cabin. Marder inhaled the rich damp air, recalled driving this car up and down the sensuous coastal curves of Highway A1A in Ft. Lauderdale during the summer of love, radio blasting, just a teenager himself, and oh, the action he'd seen. Sweet girls with sand-covered feet who whispered warm secrets and all looked like Tammys and Debbies and smelled of Coppertone and bubble gum.

But beyond that, the car merged with the memory of his father, a tall, strong man. The household of Marder's childhood had been one of divorce too, and still now he felt that loss, as though he'd never really had a father, just a weekend visitor who traveled to him in the golden car as part of an obligatory embassage and then all too soon disappeared in

52

it. Sometimes he dreamed of him standing beside the car, saw his old man handing him the keys willingly, a gift, a fantasy. He stooped, picked up the worn seat belt in his hand, wondered if his daughters felt the same way about him, or if they were inherently more secure, children of the age of guaranteed self-esteem.

"Hello, Gerry. Come to give it some exercise?" Pete, a man with a slight Greek accent and a brush-like full head of gray hair, wiped his hand on a blue rag and held it out to Marder.

"Just don't want it to get sluggish, Pete."

Pete smiled. "Uh-huh."

"Blow some of the carbon out of the exhaust system." He smoothed a hand over the freshly-waxed front fender.

Pete lifted his head back and let out a roar. "You so full of it, Gerry. You can't stay away from dis car for more den tree days. You just like teenager. Ha?"

Just like a teenager, Marder thought. "Want to keep the steel-belted tire tread even."

"You so full of it," Pete said, slapping him on the back, laughing. "Oh—say, Gerry. Dat guy, Mr. Swinlow was back."

Marder's hand came to a rest on the chrome headlight frame, where his index finger lingered—*tap, tap, tap.* "What did he want? You didn't let him drive it, did you?"

"Naw, naw. He's up to tirty-five grand, now. I told him I let you know, but dat I din tink you want to sell it."

Marder had never met this Swinlow, the auto collector, but he resented him and the temptation of his money. Made him nervous. Dream stealer.

"You did good, Pete." He wrestled off his overcoat and threw it into the passenger seat. "Don't even let him get in it, okay?"

Pete slapped Marder's back once more. "Just like teenager."

His foot slammed down on the accelerator and the dual pipes growled. *'Fierce-throated beauty!'* he thought. *Imagine the poem Whitman could have written about this.* He pushed the chrome "Wander Bar" of the radio and landed on the oldies station. Dylan's "Like A

Rolling Stone," nasal and organy, shot from the speakers.

"But Tess, I wanted you to come home for the holiday."

"Oh, Daddy—I can *always* come home. How many times can I visit Brussels?"

"How many, you mean exactly? Exactly none. I want you to come home."

Driving out toward Lindenhurst, he replayed in his head the conversation he'd had with his youngest just a few hours before, when she'd caught him in his office with a collect call from Tempe. The pain in his right side activated once again, probing, knife-like.

"Daddy—Claude's family is crazy to meet me."

"I believe the first independent clause of that statement."

"That's not fair. You know I don't understand grammar."

"Tess, no."

"Please, Daddy. Don't make me beg. I love you and I don't want to make you angry, but this is something I just have to do."

Marder had taken time out to catch his breath, to swallow a dose of Tenormin for his blood pressure, and to remember when he most wanted to do something at Tess's age when his parents wouldn't allow it, and how much it had meant to him then. What was it again? Oh, yes. Peyote.

"All right. All right, Pumpkin."

"Daddy, do you mean it?"

"Don't complicate it, now."

"Thank you, thank you, thank you! How can I thank you?"

"You can't. I don't want to be thanked. My heart isn't in this, if you'd care to know."

"I just can't believe how much I love you and how awesomely cool you are. Oh, Daddy—one more thing."

"What?"

"I need sixteen hundred dollars."

"Sixteen *hundred?* For what?"

"Airfare. It's the season"

"For Christ's sake."

"I need it today, to book the seat."

He hadn't listened to his parents, either. It had been really good peyote, too. Mexican.

◆

She would put it out of her mind for now, the sudden news of Howard's last minute trip to Atlanta during the holiday. The airport limo carrying Ophelia had just lurched up the drive, its black quarter panels stained chalk-white under layers of salt.

"It can't be helped, C-C," he'd said. "The entire land deal for the mall is at risk."

"No one does business on Christmas, Howard."

"You'd be surprised."

Yes, she would, especially after all the one-ring, hang-up phone calls she'd been receiving for how long now—six weeks? She thought of the forest green matchbook from a hotel bar that she had innocently discovered in Howard's attaché one morning while tucking in a surprise I-love-you note, back when all the trips to Atlanta had started last September. Inscribed on the inside cover was, *Carrie, 404-925-7872, call me!* When he'd returned three days later and she riffled through the attaché contents not-so-innocently, twice, the matchbook was nowhere to be found. Was she being a fool? And how would she ever know for certain? The questions floated out over the snow-blanketed yards into the colorless sky above, as her daughter, suitcase in tow, hurried up the drive, bundled in a gray-flannel coat, a green scarf knotted at her throat, riding the breeze like a pennant. Her face was just an older version of the one that belonged to the child who used to skip down the school bus steps every afternoon, and cry out, "Mommy!" She always found it an unexpected delight, something like watching a magician pull flowers from his sleeve, to see Gerry's eyes in the face of her own little girl.

And she was here now, her daughter, embracing her, the frigid blast of air from the open door bringing with it the lonely winter scent of the outdoors. Camille hung on to the cold wool of Ophelia's coat, hung on tightly, thought about how sometimes holding her own grown child was but to clasp a memory.

"I've missed you so," Camille murmured, betraying more emotion than she had intended.

"Mom—" Ophelia broke the embrace, held her mother by the shoulders at arm's length—"are you all right?"

"I'm fine, sweetheart. I'm fine—especially now that you're home."

"Oh—but I won't be home for long." She untied her scarf, flung it to the coat stand there in the foyer, missed, unbuttoned her coat. "I'm going to Vermont!"

"Vermont?"

"I mean *we're* going to Vermont, to Mount Ascutney. Me and Clifford. Remember I told you about that hunky Clifford, the one whose father practically owns the Internet?" She hung her coat and then zipped open the side pouch of her rolling suitcase. "We're going skiing. I absolutely can't ski, but I'm going anyway!"

"But honey, it's the holiday. We've been waiting for you. Tess will be in Brussels and your father—"

Ophelia kneeled before her suitcase and peered into the pouch as she pushed away cluttered items, used airline ticket stubs, nail polish, travelers size Kleenex, a paperback novel titled *Relinquished*. "Here it is. Daddy will get over it. He hates coming here anyway. Mom, I've got the best news—"

"Your father does not—"

"Yale accepted me!" Ophelia stood up, removed a letter folded in thirds from the ragged end of an envelope and held it out to her mother. "Go on. Read it!"

She took the letter in her hands, noted how old her fingers looked in contrast to her daughter's, smudged with age spots, bony. As the paper unfolded, she vaguely read the embossed letterhead, thought of the holiday dinner on the dining room table with no one gathered around it, saw Howard in a bar with a much younger woman, wondered if her life would descend into a nightmare of surreptitiously placed recording devices, private detectives. *Yale Law School. We are pleased to inform you . . . Carrie, call me!* She folded the letter, handed it back.

"Mom—you barely read it!"

"I'm so happy for you. Really. Your father will be so proud."

"Did you see the part that says I start this January? I got into the special intern thing. I'll be working with the top labor law partnership in the country. You didn't even *read* it." Her mother, she thought, looked preoccupied, eyes focused on something beyond her, something invisible. "Mother—what's wrong?"

For just a sliver of a moment Camille considered unburdening her very full heart, imagined warm sobs, the comfort of release. But that was out of the question. She had been the one to teach her daughters strength, to show them first-hand what it meant to take charge of your own life, to create options rather than brood over defeat. She put her arm around Ophelia, guided her into the living room, put on her game face. "Nothing. There's nothing in the world wrong. I was just looking forward to being with you, is all. We'll have time together when you get back from your ski trip."

"Exactly. That's the very thing I was thinking."

"Of course." Camille looked into Ophelia's eyes and saw Gerry staring back at her. She thought of that old apartment, decades ago, how neither of them knew anything when they started out, considered how brave one must be to be young. "When will you be leaving?"

"Two hours. I've got to get going!" She kissed her mother on the cheek, then kicked off her shoes and ran halfway up the stairs before remembering something important, leaning over the banister. "Oh— Mom? I'm going to need money for tuition. About fifteen grand. Can you talk to Dad for me so he doesn't have a coronary?"

Camille felt her head spin, all this commotion, expense. "But I thought you saved that money from your job."

"I did! I've even applied for my own student loans. This is Yale, Mom, not DePaul. And where's Howard?"

The phone rag. Just once.

Lana Almendinger sighed, rolled off of Marder and stretched a hand toward the package of Parliament cigarettes on the bed stand, fumbled with the crush-proof top, extracted a cigarette, struck a match, and lighted it. Marder gazed abstractedly at the smooth slope of her breast as she leaned back and pulled the bed sheets up around the olive skin of her chest walls. She was something of a beauty and he admired the youthful curves of her body, but he knew she was going to ruin the moment by talking.

"I feel the way that character feels in that Joyce Carol Oates novel. After sex, I mean. Do you know what I mean?"

Marder didn't. He wanted to tell her that fictional characters mimic real people, not the other way around. He wanted to say that he didn't like to talk about literature; he just liked reading it. He wanted to tell her to please not say anything else.

"Don't you sometimes feel like you're in the pages of a book yourself—that you, your whole life, are set in print, and that somebody else is reading about you, skimming the paragraphs that comprise your life?"

"No," Marder said. He wondered briefly what would have happened if Camille had never left him, where they would be in their lives, who would be in bed at this moment with svelte, dark-skinned Lana, who would not shut up, not even if the apocalypse suddenly ensued, would only say, "*Did you ever feel like you were in a book about the apocalypse?*" And then he ceased, because he knew about the what-if game, how sooner or later it would become a dark voyage.

Lana pulled a long strand of her hair out of her face with her cigarette hand and drew it back. "What *do* you feel like, then? You never talk."

"You take birth control, don't you?"

Lana sat up, exhaled a jet of smoke. The sheet dropped from her breasts. "Look—if you don't feel like talking, fine. I can just get dressed and catch the D train back to Brooklyn."

"I'm sorry," Marder said. "I don't know what I'm feeling. Right now I think I'm thinking more than feeling."

She pulled the blanket from the bed, furled it around her shoulders like a cape and stood, examining the contents of Marder's book cases, flicking ashes on the floor obliviously as she did so. "Like what? Tell me what you're thinking right now."

That your breasts look like pears, and now I'm going to have to vacuum the carpet. "I was thinking when we stopped, right afterward, how I wished the moment would last."

Lana paused, turned and flashed a smile at him. "Really?"

Beautiful pears. "I was wishing that *something* would last, anyway, and that it's a shame that things don't."

Camus, Tolstoy, Boyle. Lana could find no discernible order to the volumes in Marder's bookcase. "Would it be so terrible, anyway?" she asked, taking an ambitious drag on the cigarette.

"Would *what* be so terrible?"

"If I were to get pregnant, have a family."

A chill spread across his loins. Did this girl have an agenda— or could she be that innocently naïve? As she moved from Mallory to Dostoyevsky to Price, he looked at her bare feet, thought of them on the cold stainless steel of a delivery table, heard the moans of pain and anxiety, saw the stream of amniotic fluid arc over the obstetrician's shoulder. Where would her night of pleasure be then? And later would come the incessant crying, midnight feedings, sleepless nights, the inescapable resentment and fights. After work—the shuttling from day care to home, the forced civility of PTA meetings, photo albums with little frozen colorful moments pasted inside, and never quite completed. Hopes, dreams, disappointments, and suddenly all that time was gone and you were both old.

Just imagining such a thing with this girl, with anyone, other than Camille, that is, spoke of its utter impossibility. With all of the attendant sorrow and burden there was still something if not sacrosanct, then at least *special* about what they had created together, though he had to dig a good way down there before it became at all apparent.

Marder answered her question like this: "I just don't think I could do it all again."

With her smooth fingers Lana lifted a framed picture of Ophelia on a sledding hill, age nine. "Why not? You did it once."

Was she pushing the issue? A family, was that what she desired— or was this just unedited curiosity, the positing of one generation to another? "Children are wonderful. They become your whole life, and you love them. You love them so much you can't believe it. And then one day, though you thought it would never, something sinister happens. They stop being children, and they hurt you, and they leave you, and still you love them. Maybe the loss triggers a fall from grace—one of you gets greedy, for money, experience. Everyone has a little Faust in him, or her."

"Sounds like you're reliving your own marriage."

"I am. And you want me to do it again."

"I didn't *say* that. I was just asking if it would be so terrible, that's all." The phone rang. Lana crushed her cigarette out in a small robin's-egg blue ceramic thing on the bookshelf. "Do you have any beer?" she asked.

"Fridge," he replied, hand on the phone, eyes toward the thread of smoke rising from the smoldering ash in the cup that Tess had made him when she was in the third grade.

Ten minutes later, while Lana sipped a Miller's, he said goodbye to Camille, having heard all about the very lonely holiday she looked forward to, as well as Ophelia, Clifford, Vermont and the Yale acceptance, and the fifteen thousand dollars for tuition that he had three weeks to come up with. In his mind's-eye Howard-the-wife-stealing-bastard reclined in the first-class section of an airliner, sipping Dom Perignon from a long-stemmed glass, while inside the big house in Litchfield one lonely room was alight, the table covered in an elaborate white table cloth, with a single place setting.

He slowly replaced the receiver in its cradle and stared after it vacantly, thought of them, one, then another, another. A whole string. The moles on the back of Camille's thigh.

"Who was it?"

Where the hell am I going to get fifteen thousand dollars? "Hm? Oh—an old friend."

Lana picked up a photo of the golden Corvette. "Some car," she said. "Was it yours?"

Marder remembered his father behind the wheel, pulling into the driveway on a Saturday to take him bowling, saw himself, running from the house to the big man, the magic car. He shook his head. "No."

"Too bad," Lana said, sliding it back more or less in place upon the bureau. "So what do you say? You ready?"

She let the blanket fall to the floor and slowly crawled toward him upon the foot of the bed. "You know," he said, fluffing his pillows behind him, "I suddenly *do* feel like a character in a book."

Lana was upon him, warm, brown, fruity. "Which one?"

"Hector, after he's run around the wall of Troy about a dozen times, and he's ready to collapse."

"Let's make it a baker's dozen, then."

◆

Crisp, clear, December 24th came to Litchfield under a deep-blue canopy of a sky. The winter sun slipped seductively into the great room, found the terry cloth surface of Camille's robe, rubbed up against it. She stared at the telephone on the glass end table before her as if she expected it to jump up and speak to her. Her fingers interlaced, unlaced. He might have tried to cover for himself. That he could be so cavalier, or stupid—which was it? To allow the woman to answer his hotel room telephone, how could he have? Unless he hadn't time enough to stop her. Or perhaps it had been the wrong room. That was it. It must have been the wrong room.

It hadn't been the wrong room. And what was really pitiful, she thought, was the way she made up these poor excuses for him, something he wouldn't even do for himself. The great room. What was so great about it? Camille stood, walked to the floor-to-ceiling windows, considered the vaulted ceiling—showy, bourgeois. There were thousands just like it throughout Connecticut. In the corner stood the Douglas fir, still undecorated. It made her feel so blue she had to leave the room—and the one after that, dining room, living room, each clean and spacious. And empty. She ascended the spiral staircase like a human puff of smoke, drifted to the master bedroom. *How many chances do you get?* That was precisely what she had asked herself when the kids had nearly grown and Gerry lost his position and she had met Howard.

The door of Howard's walk-in closet was an enticement to do just that—walk in, and search every pocket of every suit and pair of slacks he owned for more evidence of infidelity. She touched her fingertips to the doorknobs, but was overruled by the sinking sensation in the pit of her stomach, overcome by paralysis. This was beneath her, undignified. She wanted to call up her mother, unload her soul, but her mother had been dead these past seven years. Besides, they had never really got along all that well when she had been alive. Wasn't it the truth, though—how in the long run everyone will disappoint you, even yourself? She worried for a moment about Tess, alone in Brussels, then remembered the strange woman's voice on the other end of the line—*"Hello?"*

That morning Marder roared out of Babylon for the last time. The traffic was terrible, not an open stretch of road till Route 684, where he floored the accelerator, then lightened up on it as the Vette leaned into a curve. He recalled with distaste Swinlow's attitude back in Pete's Garage. "Mr. Marder, it's to be a gift for my wife, for Christmas. It can't very well be that if she doesn't get it tomorrow."

And he'd assured him, "She'll have it tomorrow. I just need it overnight, to take it on one last trip."

"But it must be clean," Swinlow specified.

Kiss my ass, Marder thought. "I'll have it washed."

Thirty-five thousand dollars. How would he say goodbye to the car after so long? Maybe he wouldn't. Just grab the check, sign it over to Yale and not look back.

He sped past White Flower Farm, recalled the sweet, ditzy coed in his World Lit section who'd given him the drab little jar of coffee beans as a present. He felt sick when he thought about her, his own daughters, gaining experience in the world—unwanted experience, the kind that didn't do anybody any goddamn good. The exhaust rumbled while his mind played, jumped from the leaky pipe in his apartment wall to the inexact change he'd received at a newsstand, to the sad and beautiful New England snow. He wondered why his father had left his mother, why Lennon had fired his bodyguards in December of 1980, and what had caused Salinger to pack it all in and quit publishing. What a pity it all was, all the loss of sweetness.

He remembered Camille on a promontory in the botanic garden where they had spent the day twenty-five years earlier, and she had worn that blue tube top, and they had brought a picnic lunch of cheeses and sausage and some cheap wine because neither of them had known a thing about wine back then, or plants either, especially poison ivy, which they had rolled around in so amorously all afternoon. It wasn't the divorce that had hurt them, but the things that they had both allowed to happen that *led* to the divorce. And it was time, the enemy, and MTV, and Republican policies, and Democratic failures, and their own original hope that had provoked them to contribute two children to the course of history and civilization.

"It's the whole damned *world*," Marder extrapolated.

Camille lay sprawled upon the built-in leather bench by the big bay window of her room, surrounded by heaps of splayed woolen and gabardine coats and pants, heaps of them, Givenchy, Perry Ellis, Oleg Cassini, Armani, Beane, some thrown in rage against the wall, others having simply been tossed like limp designer parachutes upon the bed and armchairs, heather brown, taupe, taupe melange, oxford. In her hand were clenched another matchbook, a small note, and a business card, each with indiscreet endearments. Carrie again, and Monique, whoever she was. *Howard the cheating bastard,* she thought, without comprehending her own variation on a theme. She hadn't the heart or the will to go through his bureau. What would be the point? You get hurt, you cause hurt, you learn from your mistakes and go on. Welcome to it—life.

She cooled her aching forehead against the icy windowpane, turned her red and swollen eyes away from the sun. In the distance the town green, lying under a fresh layer of snow, touched her with its lonely beauty. Down below a serried row of icicles hung from the white wooden fence. She watched as they melted in brilliant drops into an icy pool upon the snow, watched as she lay still, prodding her heart for sensation, finding little. It reminded her of her own front yard many years ago, when she was just a girl. She had been happy then—or had she? she wondered, something catching the corner of her eye, no more

63

than a glint at first, then full-blown, the golden car turning off the roadway as if out of yesterday, into the drive.

"*Gerry Marder,*" she mouthed, squinting into the sun, remembering vividly the first time they had made love—young, sweet love, and he had recited that poem by Browning, a boat ride at night, the striking of a match. It had been May, and there had been a warm richness in the nighttime air, the scent of life and promise. He had asked her right then to marry him, that first night together, and she had held him off, because it didn't seem prudent. "Just give it some time," she had said, "a little time, is all."

The Worst Suspicions of Stanley Glickner

His wife lay curled up under the blanket and quilt of their king-size bed, with her mouth opened slightly. Every morning Stanley would peek in at her just before beginning his daily task of shaving. The covers created little mountains and valleys around her, and it was impossible for him to distinguish where at least half of her limbs were. The sun was just creeping over the horizon, and as it squeezed through the bedroom windows it added flaming touches of orange to the wrinkles of the bed covers.

Stanley walked out of the room and closed the door quietly while scratching beneath his undershirt. He glanced in at his son, Barry, who also slept with his mouth open—in the bedroom across the hall. He didn't stop or linger; instead, he walked clumsily to the bathroom and turned on the light.

He caught a glimpse of himself in the mirror just before he turned on the hot water faucet. He beamed a ridiculous grin for a second then returned to his usual sober expression, which he wore like a dull gray necktie. As he began streaking his face with foamy cream in preparation for his morning ritual, he gazed deeply into his own mousy eyes. It had become Stanley's custom to picture his own death each morning, while shaving. Yesterday he had envisioned a heart attack that he imagined would take place at his office. In the mirror he had seen, or thought that he had seen, his last personal struggle. The pain had crept down his left arm, just as he had heard that heart attacks begin. He had seen himself fall from his chair and attempt to loosen his collar, beckoning to a fellow worker whose desk was situated nearby. But his effort had been in vain. The co-worker, absorbed in business, hadn't heeded the groans, the flailing of limbs. Valiantly, Stanley Glickner had faced his last moments on earth alone.

And that was how it had happened. Yesterday, wrapped up in his vision, he had experienced death. It had been a spiritual feeling, a fantastic rush of oneness and belonging, when life seeped out.

He stared deeply at his own reflection, recalling the certainty with which he had expected to be stricken. But it never occurred. He had subsequently waited at his desk for the event, almost eagerly, the way a child feels the night before Christmas when sleep is nearly impossible. Even though the premonition had been stronger than any of the others, and even though he had pushed the papers that cluttered his desk out of his way and generally ignored the work that had piled up, it never occurred.

And so he was back at the sink on this particular morning, dragging his razor over his living face, still waiting, still staring. He rinsed the tiny hairs from his razor occasionally without looking or taking notice of the progress at hand. His wife had lately chastised him for not matching the length of his sideburns. On the left side of his face, the peninsula of hair was a good inch longer than its partner.

"I'm not a gloomy guy," he whispered to himself through lather-covered lips. "I have a good job, l love my wife, I have a normal kid—" he continued, as the next vision ensued.

A funny feeling welled up within him as he saw, far away and past the mirror, an auto on an expressway. It was a dark blue sedan with terminal rust spots, like his own. He saw himself at the wheel, driving home after a hard day at the office. He was tired and tried to loosen his tie as a big semi-trailer in front of him slammed on the brakes, jackknifed, and rolled over. Stanley felt the panic and saw the futile attempts at swerving and shifting into low gear. In a flash, the dark blue vehicle collided with several cars and the fateful truck. Those seconds came to him slowed down into sprawling minutes of struggle and then surrender, as the feeling of warmth, of belonging, smoothed over him and life seeped out once more.

"It's beautiful," he uttered, cutting his cheek with a careless twist of the razor. The absurd little grin recurred, briefly.

"Stanley!" Mrs. Glickner bellowed from downstairs. "Breakfast is ready."

He smelled the sausage and toast and instantly snapped out of his reverie.

"Stanley, would you wake up Barry? He's been late for school twice this week."

He dutifully wiped the lather from his face and walked to his son's bedroom. The boy was fast asleep, snoring at an unbelievable pitch, the result of sinus problems. Stanley pushed the boy's shoulder repeatedly.

"Your mom says it's time to get up, slugger. C'mon. She's got breakfast and everything."

Barry turned around suddenly. He was still wearing his glasses, but his father didn't notice.

"Aw, Dad! I was *asleep*!"

Nora Glickner was thirty-four years old and seldom did her nails anymore. She also seldom had her hair done, nor did she leave the house except for groceries or a rare jaunt to the post office to mail the bills. Her face betrayed the fact that she had conceded to the sameness of one day to the others. She cooked minimally, carrying her family from meal to meal on four or five recipes that she had got down to an art, though even the taste of these dishes took on a startling similarity to one another.

"Your sausages taste like your macaroni and cheese," Stanley told her, between sips of orange juice.

Nora was scraping the toast. "Look, Stanley. I don't want to hear it. Did you wake up Barry?"

"Um-hm. He said he was asleep."

"No kidding, he was asleep. The sausages taste like macaroni, I hear," his wife mimicked.

"They do," he agreed. For a moment he became lost in the piping along the front of Nora's robe. She'd been wearing that robe for close to ten years, but Stanley had just noticed the red piping, and how it ran around the collar and down the sides. "Nora, if I were to, uh—if I were to—" he stammered, as he folded up his napkin. "If something were to happen to me—"

"Oh, God. No, Stanley. Tell me you haven't been having visions again."

"Uh-huh. Just a while ago, in the mirror. Don't call them visions."

"Then what the hell are they if they're not visions?" she asked, raising her voice beyond her usual monotone.

"They're more like *suspicions*, or premonitions. I dunno. Feelings. Anyway, it's funny. I sort of think this is the one."

"I don't want to hear it."

"A car crash."

"I don't want to hear it!" she declared, emphatically.

Barry walked into the kitchen and sat down in his place between his mother and father, rubbing his eyes beneath his heavy corrective lenses. His glasses fell onto the table and he quickly retrieved them.

"Dad, what doesn't Mom want to hear?"

"Nothing. Eat your macaroni."

"Huh?" The confused boy stared down at his sausage and toast.

Nora stood up and brought her plate to the sink. She ran the water, picked up a dish towel, and stared out the window into the front yard.

"Barry," she started, "tell your father what you told me last night after you finished your homework."

Barry smiled rarely, but at odd moments he beamed a ridiculous grin. He played with half a sausage, using his fork as a hockey stick. The improvised puck flew across the table and dropped to the floor.

"Aw, Mom. I'm *eating*!"

"Go ahead. Tell him," Nora insisted.

Barry looked up at his father and said, "Nothing. I just keep thinking that my arm is gonna get broke."

◆

Stanley departed from his normal lunchtime routine that day. It had become his habit to catch a snack at a small restaurant called Mary's Beef, though her hash browns were quickly growing indistinguishable from her hamburgers. He walked instead to a temple in the vicinity of his office to keep an appointment he had made that morning with a rabbi. Stanley was by no means *very* religious, though he regarded himself as *slightly* religious at times, in his own peculiar way. His preoccupation with death was surely a sign of his awareness of the brevity and beauty of life, he liked to believe. This meeting, this impending talk with a rabbi was to his mind a sort of life insurance designed to clean up any loose philosophical ends. He believed without a doubt that he would find himself driving dangerously near to a semitrailer that afternoon on his way home.

Though it was a city temple on Chicago's near-north side, it kept the atmosphere of a pastoral estate. The grounds were on the lavish side, and the path to the main entrance was surrounded by shrubbery and flowers.

"I'm not a gloomy guy," Stanley said to himself, as he began climbing the dozen or so stairs to the door. He noticed a gardener, a man with a tan cap and a gray mustache, staring at him. Stanley nodded. The old man continued to plant a rosebush, a job he went about with studied patience and care.

He met Rabbi Jacobson in his library and shook hands with him a bit longer than necessary. He went to glance at his wristwatch self-consciously only to find that he had left it at home on his dresser.

"What can I do for you, Mr. Glickner?" Rabbi Jacobson asked, with gravity.

"Stanley."

"Hm?" the rabbi inquired.

"Call me Stanley."

"All right, Stanley. What can I do for you?"

Stanley proceeded to narrate his morning suspicions to Rabbi Jacobson, while pulling absently at an unraveled thread in his suit coat. He told the man of his certainty of death, of the spiritual feelings he anticipated at the last moments, and of the rushing completeness that followed. The rabbi listened with an intent expression and nodded frequently.

"Don't you think that's how it must be?" Stanley asked. "Don't you suppose it's fulfilling and peaceful?"

"I suspect, Mr. Glickner—"

"Stanley. Call me Stanley."

"All right, Stanley. I suspect it is something like that. However, I think you are letting life pass by with all this worry about the end. You are not enjoying the in-between."

"Oh, I'm not worried. I'm just certain."

"Good. As long as you're not worried, why not enjoy? What can we know with certainty, I ask you? We know very little with *certainty*. This fetish of yours, this vision of your death is not bad in and of itself—so long as it doesn't interfere with your usefulness. So long as your family doesn't feel a burden as a result of your fascination with your final end. From what you tell me, this is not your first—uh—suspicion."

"Uh-uh. I was supposed to have a heart attack yesterday."

"But did you?"

"Uh-uh."

"That's my point, Mr. Glickner. Stanley. You're still here in one piece. Enough of this morbid talk. You are a *mensch*. Act like a *mensch*. No more of this gloominess."

"I'm not a gloomy guy," Stanley agreed.

"Of course you're not! When death comes, it will be as you say; I'm sure. A moment of meaning, of oneness. But so too can your life, Stanley Glicken, be a time of meaning."

"Glickner."

Hm?" the rabbi asked.

"Glickner. My last name is Glickner."

"Well, I've enjoyed talking with you, Stanley. Go out and breathe the air. Smell the flowers. This is a time of life."

Stanley thanked Rabbi Jacobson graciously, though briefly. As he walked outside he felt like a new man. He took a deep breath and smiled, not so ridiculously, as he skipped down the steps. He stopped next to the gardener and enjoyed the planting of the rosebush with the old man.

"That," said Stanley, "is a beautiful rosebush."

"Yes it is, young man. It's a work of true beauty—but it sure is hell getting it to stand right."

Stanley watched him pat the earth into place with his bare hands.

"You know," Stanley began, "I came here thinking about death, and now all I can think about is life."

The old man struggled to his feet and wiped some sweat from his forehead with his sleeve.

"You talked to Rabbi Jacobson?"

"Uh-huh. I'm gonna start living today."

"That's good," said the old man. "Rabbi Jacobson is the finest."

"Yeah. Say, do you ever think about what death must be like?"

The gardener stuck a soiled finger in his mouth and released the air in a *pop!*—like the sound a cork makes when it is pulled from a bottle.

"Just like that," said the old man.

Stanley stared for a second. "Hm. I was telling the rabbi that I think of it as a fulfillment. You know, like a significant—"

Pop! The gardener made the sound again and went off to plant another rosebush.

Stanley was too joyous to let the difference in opinion bother him. He nurtured something new in his heart as he strolled back to the office, a feeling of contentment and peace. The preeminence of life was everywhere. He found plain women attractive, and the obnoxious panhandlers who congregated on Rush Street were considerably less obnoxious—nearly tolerable, in fact. Every nuance of pleasantness was visible to him, and he praised the windfall that had led him to this new plateau. Rabbi Jacobson was indeed quite a man.

So animated was Stanley, that when Mrs. Orbison, the sad old receptionist for the insurance firm at which he worked, asked him for the three thousand and fifty-first time, "How's life, Stanley?" he kissed her.

"Life's beautiful, Mrs. Orbison. As beautiful as you are."

She stared after him and sniffed for telltale signs of alcohol.

Once seated at his desk, he pushed the remaining papers to the side and quickly punched the familiar number of his home phone.

"Hello?" Nora answered, sounding strangely distracted.

"Nora? Stanley. God, is it good to hear your voice!"

"Stanley, not now. Jesus, not now."

"Yes, *now*, Nora. You'll never in a million years guess what's happened to me. I feel so damn good I want to tell the world. I made an appointment today—"

Nora interrupted her exuberant husband. "Look, in case you're interested—"

"I am, I am! But listen, Nora. I made an appointment with a rabbi—Rabbi Jacobson, at Beth Or. He's changed my life. I told him about the death thing and he assured me that death *will* be important. It *will* be meaningful. But God, he opened my eyes to *life*. He made me realize about the in-between, the now. I never felt so good in all my life!" He sat back in his chair and placed his feet informally upon his desk. "I love you, Nora," he said, at last.

"Barry broke his arm at school today. Stanley? Did you hear me? You know that arm he's been having funny feelings about? Of course, *you* wouldn't know where he got *those* ideas, would you, Stanley?"

There was silence on the line for a second as Stanley stared transfixedly into space. Then Nora hung up. His smile faded as he sat motionless with the receiver suspended an inch or so from his ear. He slowly removed his feet from his desk and dropped the phone to the floor. Grabbing his briefcase, Stanley walked briskly out of the office, past the still-wary receptionist. He rang for an elevator and waited impatiently, pushing the "down" button several times. After what seemed like a lifetime, the doors opened and Stanley boarded. At the ground floor he beelined through the revolving door and ran toward LaSalle Street, to the garage where his car was parked.

It was precisely 2:13 p.m. when Stanley loosened his tie, rushed into the street, and was crushed by the LaSalle bus. One witness, an old woman who made the six o'clock news that night, said it was the dumbest thing she had ever seen. When the reporter asked her if she remembered any details, anything at all, the old woman stuck a gnarled finger in her mouth and released the air in a pop.

"That was it," she said. "He just went *pop!*"

La Belle Dame sans Merci

Part I: Forgetting John Keats

Thwack! The tennis ball shoots diagonally, is struck again, lobs lazily over the net, causing Aaron to hasten to it, presenting him with a timely opportunity to show off his finest tennis choreography, knees bent, broad shoulders pivoting as he backhands the DayGlo orb, sending it in a lazy arc over Julia's head.

I don't play tennis. Instead I watch my girlfriend play tennis with her boss, a man who, next year, is likely to be one of the most important legislators in the state of Illinois. For just a freeze-frame moment he looks like an imitation of one of his own campaign photographs. The victor. Julia meets him at the net to concede, her smooth arms and legs still May-pale. By July she will be bronze, and when she wears white she will look like a magazine ad for the Cayman Islands, the way she did last summer when we first met at the athletic club. Aaron's hair is cut short, catches the ever-so-slight breeze. His teeth are all even and brilliantly white. When he smiles he could blind you.

"You shouldn't have been able to make that last shot," Julia teases. "It was a technical impossibility."

"I specialize in the impossible," he says.

Julia says, "That's just another way of saying you're lucky, is all."

"*Luck*, my dear, is a word the defeated use to account for the winner's skill." He flashes his campaign grin at me. "What do you say, Tom? Was it luck, or did I have the obvious advantage?"

"I'm afraid I didn't notice," I say, indicating with a tip of my head

73

the twenty or so un-graded essays on the spectator bench beside me. "But I know you've had all kinds of advantages."

Julia tilts her sun visor up and lets her hand rest on my shoulder.

"Sour grapes," Aaron says. "You're a couple of sour grapes, the two of you. Julia, you'll see to the Greenberger papers this afternoon?"

"I've already called ahead to the office. Stacy's on it right now."

"Good. Make sure she stays on it. I want those delivered by messenger today." And then to me: "So long, *professore*. Learn them kids good."

I have a momentary fantasy of murdering him with his own tennis racquet. I can think of at least three ways to do it.

We lunch at The Grille in Lake Forest. The waitress has brought me an uncommonly well-made Bloody Mary. Two green olives, a black one, a pickle spear, generous portion of vodka. *God bless that girl*, I think.

"You ought to be kinder to Aaron," Julia tells me, from relatively out of the blue. "He picks up on your sarcasm, you know."

"He's that advanced, is he?" She shoots me a look of disapproval across the table, one, I take it, that she has learned from her mother. Her mother was the last one I saw use it, right after we were introduced. "Besides, I thought all he picked up was other guys' girls."

Julia stirs her salad obliviously with her fork. "We're not going over your silly jealousies again. Aaron is the most progressive candidate in the state, and he's going to win the election." Around and around the lettuce spins on her plate, a tiny green galaxy. "And when he does, we're moving to Springfield. What you need to do is stop procrastinating, and start writing your dissertation. Get it over with."

When I first laid eyes on Julia it was something like being electrocuted. In a good way. She was running on a treadmill, and I'd just walked into the gym from the locker room. What first caught me were her eyes, large and bright, and her strength and stature. *Breeding*, I thought, an unusual term to apply to a person, or maybe not. It was almost as though her family's wealth was genetic in nature, monetary ripples just beneath her pecs, part of the package.

Julia is the package, the whole package. And what is one to

do when gifted with a package? I've been unwrapping Julia since last August, and I keep looking to see what might be inside.

My straw makes sucking noises. All gone. The ice cubes run aground. I say, "We haven't had the Springfield discussion yet."

"That's because there's nothing to discuss. Aaron wins the election, we move to Springfield, and I run his office. You can always get an adjunct position somewhere, till you get your Ph.D."

I stare over Julia's shoulder, through the front window. A man gets into a silver-gray Maserati, backs into traffic, and zooms away. Just like that. I wonder how someone gets to that point in life. You could buy a condo for the money.

I don't tell Julia that the problem with progressive politicians is that they are still politicians. I don't tell her that I've already made an appointment for tomorrow with Dr. Sommerdale, my dissertation advisor. I don't tell Julia a lot of things.

The click of my heels upon the scuffed linoleum floor echoes off the painted cinderblock walls. Here and there flyers taped at chance angles advertise club meetings, tutoring at discount prices, student concerts. One reads *Dare to Live Today*, a lecture series. Down the dimly lit hall a young woman practices musical scales discordantly on a violin, and I want to tell her that I am too old for this, for any of this, thirty-one on my next birthday, and that really she ought to stop that awful screeching, right now, please.

When at last I am sitting before Dr. Sommerdale, I can't take my eyes from a small piece of netting that has escaped like a tiny traitor from beneath the widow's peak of his hairpiece. His office is closet-small and there is not a smidgen of breeze, of anything that remotely resembles ventilation.

"Mr. O'Connell—" He prefaces every sentence with my surname. "—your dedication to the subject of Keats and your knowledge of his letters are admirable indeed, but this notion that you can determine what his mature world view and philosophy might have been, had he lived, is . . . well, problematic, to say the least. I'd nearly rather suffer another lurid study on his relationship with that Brawne woman, though it's been done to death. Everyone these days is Keats-crazy. I still haven't forgiven him for 'Endymion.' What a lot of sheer rubbish *that* was. He should have been horsewhipped!"

"Dr. Sommerdale, he was dying of con*sump*tion."

"Well, don't look at me that way, my boy. *I* didn't give it to him!" And with this he leans back in his chair, closes his eyes, and is lost in a euphoria of un-pent cackles and chortles for fully a minute or more. When at last he comes out of it, his cheeks reddened, his forefinger wiping stray tears from the corners of his sagging old eyes, he suggests, out of breath, "Mr. O'Connell, now, really, Byron is greatly superior to your cockney friend. Wouldn't you rather do a bell-ringer of a dissertation on him?"

The netting. I am tempted to reach my fingers to his forehead and tuck it under the old moth-eaten toupee. Either that or rip it off his head and go running down the hall, scare the violinist with it.

When I tell him no, he brings both his hands down in fists upon his desk blotter, as though he might beat me till I change my topic proposal. Then in one movement he picks up a fountain pen, uncaps it with his thumb, and begins writing furiously something in large, florid script. If he had produced a quill, an inkpot, and a bottle of laudanum, it would not have surprised me. Upon completion, he slides the paper across his desk to me. It reads: *The Dark Age of John Keats.*

I say, "What's this?"

"That is the new title of your dissertation."

"But what does it mean?"

"You are going to chronicle, in scholarly detail, the manner in which John Keats was forgotten during an entire generation, before he was rediscovered, and before all those later editions and adaptations of that damnable poem, the one with Porphyro hiding in the closet, what's it called—"

"The Eve of St. Agnes."

"Precisely. Now off with you. It's time for research."

It's time for beer, I think, more to the point. I drive my navy blue Geo Metro to Lake Forest's The Lantern, and begin my tour of world beers. I am soon in Belgium, drinking a Stella Artois, and looking forward to The Netherlands, and a pint of Brand. By the time I make it to Germany, I know (after grading another essay on "How to Build Your Own Computer") that I do not want to beg for my choice of study.

I am discovering myself though negation. I do not want to go to Springfield. I do not want Aaron even vaguely associated with my life. Somewhat stunned, I realize that I am growing indifferent toward Julia—beautiful, strong, well-bred Julia. What in God's name *do* I want? Perhaps the answer is in Prague. Not in Prague *per se*, but in a Czechoslovakian beer.

No, it isn't there. I leave my car on the street and walk home; I might not know what I want, but I know I am past my limit, in danger of having my drinking passport revoked.

◆

This morning I am in the university library, eating chocolate bars (a tobacco substitute) and reading all I can find about Keats's death and the days to come. It will probably take me years if I go through with this—the letters of his circle, Charles Brown, his beloved Fanny Brawne ("*That Brawne woman*," as Dr. Sommerdale referred to her), Joseph Severn. Ah—Severn. Severn the painter, the faithful friend, kind and caring to the end. Keats practically coughed himself to pieces in Severn's arms—Severn had not a thought for his own welfare, for the very real danger that he may himself contract consumption. All those days and nights locked up in their little place in the Piazza di Spagna, Keats half in love with death because he knew he could never grow to be the poet that he was certain that he might have been. I need to know what he was thinking, what he wanted to write now that he could write no more.

I slam shut the volume that I have been reading. One hour till my 101 section, and still four or five papers to go. I brush through one called "Making a Killing on eBay," and another, "Changing Your Car's Oil Is an Art Form." I jot notes about tense consistency, the use of objective case pronouns. I unwrap a Hershey's Milk Chocolate and devour it in one, two bites.

Then there is an essay called "Hina Matsuri and The Japanese Day of Re-birth." The student—Akemi Morioka. I am transported to Japan during the month of March. Spring comes early, "delicately upon the sensibilities of young girls, ardent to share their Hina-ningyo with family and visitors alike." A set of fifteen dolls in ancient ceremonial costumes is laid out upon the steps of a little house. An emperor, some musicians, ladies, ministers— there is an empress, also. As Akemi puts it, "The emperor has a grave air of dignity in contrast to the fragile, light days of the new and fresh season. Springtime make my heart feel as though tiny sparrow birds dance within it."

The vaulted ceiling of the library has not crashed down upon me, and that fact alone comes as a shock, for what are architectural principles compared to the explosion of words that I have just read on this plain, white page? How do the joints stay fixed in place, secured, in the presence of such simple, honest beauty? What are they against the elegance of Akemi's "Hina Matsuri"?

◆

I met a lady in the meads,
Full beautiful—a faery's child,
Her hair was long, her foot was light,
And her eyes were wild.

It is the summer session of English 101, section 007, a rhetoric class. We have spent two weeks on modes of writing—narrative, process, and extended definition. Without any warning, I give a seminar on British romantic poetry, focusing on Keats's ballad, "La Belle Dame sans Merci." Four or five confused students give me the shady looks I have coming. Most of the others couldn't care less if I were talking about transitions or past participles. What I try very hard not to do is take in the details of Akemi Morioka's face, which are finely sculpted, animated, as though she can barely contain her enthusiasm for life, a spiritual radiance which is natural, but nearly blinding. All this I skim from the corners of my eyes. I wonder how I could have failed to notice her before.

Have I mentioned that I quit smoking? I quit twice last month and once this week.

"Mr. O'Connell," an impatient objection from a tall youth with a ponytail. He sits in the corner and grimaces at me, most of the time. He has clearly had enough.

"Yes—Jason, is it?"

"Jordan."

"Of course, Jordan."

"I don't want to sound rude or anything, but what's all this poetic stuff got to do with extended definition?"

An unsettling rustle of voices follows. I recognize it as the prelude to a mutiny.

I say, "Jordan, you like baseball, don't you?"

He shuffles his feet, which are ensconced in big, brown lace-up boots beneath his desk. "Well, yeah."

"Think of it like that, then. Curve ball. Change of pace."

After class I sit alone in the adjunct office, reading a letter from Keats to Fanny Brawne, date uncertain, perhaps July 15, 1819. It is an embarrassing series of confessions, and he complains that she is disinterested in him, but he tries to make it sound as though he is not carping, rather carrying a kind of cross of the heart. There are times (like this) that I could grab the ailing Keats by the collar, shake him, perhaps even slap him across his face—lightly, just to get his attention. *"Do not let her do this to you!"* I want to say.

There is a knock upon the open door, a slight rapping, three times. I look up, and it is Akemi.

"Professor?" she says. I shoot to my feet, dropping the volume closed.

"Akemi," I say. "Come in, come in." There is no chair for her, so I slide one out from the desk next to mine, wheel it just before her, extend my hand in a manner of invitation.

"I hope I am not troubling you," she says.

79

No, no trouble, I assure her. There is that flashing about her again, an effulgence, and I discover that it comes from her eyes. She is a slender woman of about, what—twenty-nine, thirty, perhaps?—although there is a timeless beauty in the features of her face. And she wants to know if she is troubling me.

She sits, then flicks through the pages of her notebook till she finds what she is looking for—the handout of "La Belle Dame sans Merci," the poem that I presented in class. She places it upon my desk, and very deliberately, with great purpose, she traces the lines of a stanza with her delicate forefinger, and searches my face with her eyes to see if I comprehend her concern, the import that lies there.

> *I saw pale kings and princes too,*
>   *Pale warriors, death-pale were they all;*
> *Who cry'd— 'La Belle Dame sans Merci*
>   *Hath thee in thrall!'*

I nod a few times, uncertain, and she nods with me, as if that will help me understand.

"I see, Akemi. But what is it?"

Her mouth purses in a momentary "o" shape. Then: "She has stolen his *heart*."

And so I will have to start smoking again tonight, this afternoon, as soon as possible.

"Yes, she has. That's very good, Akemi. That is exactly what she has done."

That appears to be all there is to it. She nods once more, gravely this time, and places the poem back in her folder, as if returning a valuable document to its place. She stands. I stand.

She begins to leave, but then turns suddenly, her eyes enunciating a question before her lips can catch up. "She is not a *bad* woman?" She asks this as if she wants assurance.

"No," I say, "she is not bad. She is mysterious, and she is very beautiful, perhaps of a different world."

And then—and this is completely unexpected—she bows to

me. Out of reflex, and a great deal of appreciation and awe, I bow back. Two, three times we perform this gesture, and then she is gone. Just the silence of the room punctuates her absence. There is half a package of cigarettes in my briefcase.

"You have to start taking this seriously, Tom. Think of it as a business merger."

I have stopped by The Deer Path Inn, an old, stately hotel and restaurant, for one drink with Julia, and to cancel our plans for this evening—all those English 101 papers. We were supposed to see a concert. She is not pleased.

I sip my wine. I slip a Three Musketeers bar from the breast pocket of my sport coat. "Let me see if I get this straight. Getting married is like a business merger?"

"In every way. Two entities joined together, getting tax breaks, compounding capital, sharing assets, a common goal."

"You romantic, you. Sounds like Aaron's version of love."

She stirs the ice cubes of her cocktail irritably, avoiding my eyes. "Aaron leads an entire county. He makes plans and gets things done. All I know is, you and I need to settle our future, and only one of us is trying."

Settle the future. I wonder how it is that you go about getting the future to agree to your terms, to turn out exactly the way you want it to.

I say, "Buy a Prius? Build a McMansion in the suburbs?"

Julia bristles. "What's wrong with an environmentally friendly car, and a home in a safe place?"

I am half a world away as I ask, "Did you ever have dolls as a child?"

She folds her napkin, places it squarely upon the table, lifting her purse from the floor. The evening is over. "I'm talking about our lives, and you're eating candy and talking about toys. I make plans, and you break them. And when do you suppose we'll get another opportunity to see James Taylor at Ravinia?"

With any luck, we won't.

◆

In Rome, lying in his little room, feverish, despondent, Keats refused to open the letters from Fanny. He would see the shape and color of the wax seal, know it was hers, and look away. Had her flirtations, her apathy so destroyed him? Or was it like his writing itself—which he had also come to neglect . . . a love that had no future because *he* had no future? Had he finally floundered upon something that even his great imagination could not transcend or bridge?

I read right on the floor between the stacks up on the second floor of the library, reclining my spine against the shelves till it aches. Poor Keats—sallow, perspiring through his English cotton shirt, the coarse wool of his only suit. Mother gone. Brother gone. A thousand miles interceding between himself and his beloved. His dream of being a great poet—an eternity away. But which mattered most—his lost love, or his ruined art?

Today I have prepared a lesson on "Lamia" for my confused and unsuspecting students. Lamia, Keats's strange female vampire-serpent, disguised as a beautiful woman. She enchants and seduces. She could probably manage state political campaigns. But after I carefully set my text upon the podium and look out at the class, there is an immediate and conspicuous absence, one that, for me, at least, might as well be a rip in the fabric of the space-time continuum.

No Akemi.

And so I give an improvisational lesson on extended definitions of abstract concepts—loneliness, for instance. Emptiness. Confusion. Class runs short and I return to the shabby shelter of the adjunct office. Beside me is a worn copy of *The Oxford English Dictionary*, one that has been duct-taped along its spine. The only other presence in the office is old, retired Dr. Reemers, who plays chess against a computer software program for hours at a time. Strategic intellectual masturbation. *How does someone end up like that*? I wonder.

It is nothing, a chance discovery, as I mechanically check my email: an ad for instant hair re-growth, another urging me to sell my precious metal, some pornography that got past the university spam catcher. And just beneath that—"From your student, Akemi Morioka." I click it open at once.

> Dear Mr. O'Connell, Sir,
>
> This is your student, Akemi Morioka, with news I
> wish not may disappoint you. It sadden to say I had
> to return to my family's home in Tokyo to care for my
> ailing auntie. I will email my definition paper to you,
> if you find the practice acceptable. Perhaps I return
> to the United States sometime, but for now I must
> remain. I hope my letter finds you in good health,
> and that you approve of my essay. I use the Japanese-
> English dictionary unsparingly.
>
> I will always treasure memories of your class, and your
> helpful direction.
>
> Yours,
> Akemi Morioka

I read it twice. Then again, this time taking apart each sentence, reading each word with the inflection Akemi would have given it, hearing the gentle music of her voice. Soon I feel as though "little sparrow birds dance in my heart," to quote a great, but as of yet, undiscovered poet.

In the far corner of the office Dr. Reemers has just checkmated himself.

My apartment is tiny—a two-floor walk-up. Across the train tracks outside my window is the house in which Genevra King grew up, the girl who spurned F. Scott Fitzgerald and by doing so shot him to lofty literary heights, telling him that rich girls do not marry poor boys. It is for sale, the house. It can be yours for six million dollars. A steal.

I am surrounded by books—books on the floor, the coffee table, the tiny kitchenette counters. Keats, Keats, and more Keats. I read on the floor, curled up on a worn rug. Paisley pattern. Looks like it has thrown up upon itself. Once Fanny got word of Keats's death, she shut herself off in some kind of self-imposed house seclusion for about two weeks, and then never mentioned him again, except in rare instances. Word got around in poetic circles that Keats had been smitten by some mysterious *femme fatale*—inspired at first, and then struck dead of a broken heart. The truth was something else again. Fanny was a mousy little thing of no distinguishing grace or beauty who enjoyed minor league coquetry at military balls. While Keats, increasingly subscribing to a Platonic concept of artist-as-receptacle-of -the-divine, literally bled to attain poetic immortality, Fanny wanted to boogie.

But she had kept Keats's love letters.

I light a cigarette. All out of chocolate. I can always quit again tomorrow. Fanny is partially redeemed—until I open another volume and discover that she instructed her son to sell the letters after her death. They would get a good price on the market. Keats had no offspring to benefit financially from the expressions of his great love and desire. The beneficiary was a subsidiary of an entirely different merger.

Of course now, one must take into account Fanny's young age. She was just a girl, and genius can be a burden. What did she know of the pangs that send an artist (even if that artist sees himself as nothing more than the agent of divinity) on a quest for beauty? And for how long could Keats have kept up that intense level of passion?

I think of Julia, see her in the future in a green suburb, in a newly built house with the obligatory bourgeois turret. I look for myself in this mental picture and wonder where I may be—perhaps in the den, penning a brilliant analysis of "Hyperion," or else sold off into indentured servitude to sustain the weight of the mortgage.

There is another book I have borrowed from the library, *Leave Your Shoes at the Door: How to Avoid Culture Shock in Japan*. It is my new constant companion, worth its weight in yen, which, I learn, is pronounced *en*. Should a funeral car pass you, you must hide your thumbs. And how about this—in Japan you do not take a bath to get clean. You sponge bathe yourself and rinse and then get in the bathtub—

to *soak*. The number four is considered bad luck; it is pronounced like the word for death.

A-ke-mi Mor-i-o-ka. It is not so much a name as a melody.

◆

"Tom? Do you know what time it is?"

I am standing at Julia's apartment door, which she keeps half-closed behind her, her naked foot propped against it. I am not entirely sure why I have come here, though I think it has something to do with the rising sun and travel.

"Tom?"

"It's two in the morning," I say.

From inside, Aaron calls her name languidly, with just the slightest hint of a question at the end. We stare at one another. Julia's face slowly droops from the expectant cover-up freeze. "I didn't mean for this to happen," she says to me.

I do not know what to think of this development, whether I should walk away in a huff, go inside and use it as a good excuse to murder the bastard, or congratulate her. There will be no merger after all. A friendly takeover has transpired. The commerce of love.

"What the hell," I say. "A girl's got to dance, right?"

Her foot moves slightly and the door closes. She folds her arms across her chest, narrows her eyes. "What is that supposed to mean?"

"Nothing," I say. It's just something I read."

I am halfway down the hallway stairs when I hear her call, "But what will you *do*?"

She means without her, I realize. Julia cannot fathom anyone's world without her. But I can. At last, I can.

Outside the dark morning air is cool. I walk alone down a sidewalk, the world unconscious behind closed doors. Well, most of the world. I discover a spare Almond Joy in the pocket of my windbreaker. If it weren't only done in musicals, I might click my heels.

◆

You mustn't do anything rash, I tell myself, as I book one-way passage to Tokyo on the Far East Airlines Internet web site. It is a very good price, and so I compliment myself on keeping my head. I am wonderfully calm. Wonderfully, ecstatically, wildly calm. Next, I write a note to the Dean, explaining that a family emergency has come up—which is true. It's Akemi's family, but he does not need to know that.

The landlord—oh, hang the landlord. He can keep my furniture in lieu of the six months rent I owe on the lease. It's worth less than half of that, but let him try to find me in Tokyo.

I wonder how long Julia has been sleeping with Aaron, surprised at a sudden ember of jealousy. *No matter*, I tell myself. *Don't go down that road now, of all times.*

And so, dear Akemi, unexpected business brings me
to your city. I do hope that you will be able to find
time to perhaps be my guide as I learn my way around
Kotoku, near your auntie's home, discovering the fine
points of your rich culture.

Your presence in my class and in my heart will always
be a golden treasure.

Yours,
Tom O'Connell

I hit the *send* button, aware that I have just altered the trajectory of my life's orbit forever—an astronaut of love. How magnificent the world looks from up here—all mine again.

The Artistic World View of the Mature Poet, John Keats
Dr. Sommerdale fingers the document hesitantly, as if someone had just placed a fresh turd before him. His eyes, overly moist and swollen with age, look up from the paper to me.

"Tell me what it is that I'm looking at, Mr. O'Connell."

"The title of my dissertation," I say, "which, by the way, my entire oversight committee has approved, with the exception of you, that is."

"You got Dandler and Wycroft to sign off on this?"

"Yes, sir."

He mumbles something indistinct, nods to himself, and pushes the paper a good way across the scarred grain of his old mahogany desk.

"My boy," he says, almost apologetically, straining as if to help get the heft of his meaning across, "it's just that I don't see how you can establish what *would* have been if it never *was*."

Today his toupee is a touch off kilter, the netting once again fully exposed. He starts slightly as I reach out and tuck the fabric beneath the hairline, and pat it in place.

"Why, Dr. Sommerdale, with all due respect—sometimes the only way we *can* know what might have been is if it never was."

Like that mental picture of Julia's future house, for instance, the one with the phony turret and all that green lawn, I think to myself. *No wonder I was never able to find myself in it.*

I consider for a moment that I do not deserve this happiness. But yes, I do. Certainly I do. It's amazing how many socks with holes I have in my dresser. Out they go. I would be laughed out of Japan in those things, my brogues parked at the front door. And now with the full committee's approval, I will keep Keats alive. Gasping and hacking, but alive in the hearts and minds of readers forever. *Sayonara, English 101 students. Goodbye, old Dr. Sommerdale. Balls to you, Aaron. Ohayoo gozaimasu, Tokyo!*

I lay down a final item in the scarce room of one of my bags, a Hina-ningyo doll I have purchased, a gift for Akemi. It is an empress in a red wedding kimono, elegant, her face stoic beneath a striking silver hat, white as a kabuki player. *My dearest lady,* I rehearse as a salutation, for when I appear at her aunt's door, shoes in hand. It is a greeting that Keats sometimes used in his letters to Fanny. Or is that too formal? *My dearest Girl,* another of Keats's. That's it. The tenor is so important, the fine points of personal communication precise in their intent. The kimono is a subtle detail, I think, though unmistakable. In any case I can always claim I did not know it was ceremonial wedding garb.

On my laptop I save as a favorite site an English library page I will use while I write my dissertation in the mornings, over tea, no doubt. In the afternoons, the Japanese air faintly scented with blossoms, Akemi and I will take long walks, and I will learn of her childhood, her dreams of the future, her desires, though I believe those are hardly hidden or arcane.

A tone sounds from the computer. I have new email. The click of the mouse, solitary, final. *Akemi!* I think, and my heart lifts, until all too soon, it falls.

Mr. O'Connell, Sir—

As much as I truly would like to honor your request to serve as your guide in my city, I am sorry to tell I will be unable. My husband's United States visa have expired and may not be renewed at this time. He come to join me in caring for my auntie, and I must also assist him to find suitable position in his field of engineering.

Fervently I wish that your time in Tokyo is pleasant, and that you obtain a guide suitable to your needs. Have safety in your travels.

Fondly,
Akemi

I stare at the computer, my gaze abstracting, until the Times New Roman letters become nothing more than dancing random black shapes upon the screen, the room lit by its white glare. After several moments I see that there is an addendum at the end of the note, just the tops of the words visible, petals on the surface of a pond, until I scroll down.

P.S. Professor—perhaps the faery child lady did not intend to steal the heart of the knight at arms. Perhaps it were accident.

Part II: Some Time on the Mersey

George and Georgiana Keats arrived at the Crown Inn, Liverpool, on
23 June, 1818, a day before George's brother, John, was set to begin
his walking trip north with his good friend, Charles Brown. These are the
facts, but they do nothing to illustrate the subtext of these people's lives,
which was emotionally charged, discordant, volatile. George had not
earlier carefully or fully considered what emigrating to America would
mean to his young wife, the separation anxiety she would experience, the
result of being away from her family for so long, an uncertain future in
Louisville, Kentucky looming before her like a gathering thunderhead
on the western horizon. Neither had he counted on Brown becoming so
important in the life of his brother, almost as though he were stepping in
to take his own place, filling the vacancy before it emerged. Something
about Brown's attitude chafed at him too, a steely look of disapproval that
he could not account for, unless—

Unless John had confided in him the business about the loan of
his portion of the inheritance. How else could he have afforded to book
passage on The Telegraph, the swift sailing vessel that would take him and
his new bride to America in record time, eight weeks? And in high style
as well, having rented one of only two available cabins, each consisting of
twin rooms, the other booked by Americans known only as Aaron and
Julia, the exact nature of their relationship undisclosed. George wondered,
Would he have been so indiscreet, my own brother? Are they really that
close, he and Brown? Though to simply watch them, and listen, to take
in the easily exchanged words that flowed so smoothly between them—
as if choreographed in advance, yet natural, as though one mind was
conversing with itself, or an individual with his twin—made the answer

plain. He was jealous of their rapport, for it excluded him, and redoubled his feelings of loss, of departure, even before he had taken his leave of land and begun his voyage. But even more his discomfort was directly linked to the transparency of his situation if indeed knowledge of the loan had become common. Whom could he trust?

And John, John Keats, aware not only of the tremendous strain his upcoming walking tour with Brown would put on his tenuous stamina, but also cognizant of the portentous nature of his recent decision to turn his back on his medical career for a life of letters, must have felt a great burden, especially because he had presaged the savage reviews his recent volume of poetry would generate. To add to his habitual uneasiness over the safety of his siblings, he now carried new fears about his brother Tom's health, George's and Georgiana's uncertain travels, and the distance that would intercede between them, especially in regard to Georgiana, or Georgie, as he liked to call her.

If nothing else, embarking with Brown early the next morning on their northern route would keep him busy with purpose, too busy to allow himself to wallow in care and disquiet, as he usually did during extended periods of solitude and inertia.

I lower my glasses and rub the sleep out of my eyes, leaning back in my leather chair, one of the arms of which is worn through to the foam padding. I should get a new chair. The problem is, I'm allowing myself to wallow in care and disquiet during an extended period of solitude and inertia. It has been fifteen days since I realized that I was in love with Akemi Morioka, a twenty-nine year old student in my English 101 class, the same day I discovered that she had a husband, and had flown back to Tokyo to be with him.

So I work on my dissertation. I snoop on the secret life of John Keats, hoping I can trace the development of his mature philosophical take on not only literature, but life itself. However, I am finding more than I hoped to uncover—and not just that seething distrust between Brown and Keats's brother George, though that is intriguing because of one of its implications. Maybe I have a dirty mind (*maybe?*), but I have come across several references to Brown's affection for Keats. Yes, *affection.* What sort of affection? Filial? Platonic? I do not know. I have not determined yet. Leave that alone for now. I *do* know that later after the walking trip had been aborted in Inverness, Brown's voice was one of the loudest and clearest when it came to trying to dissuade Keats from his obsession with Fanny. In fact, Keats expressed to Brown his distrust of and dislike for women in general on more than one occasion, and he found an ardent listener there. And now I must deal with *that* dynamic in the fabric of my studies as well, but it's not my real interest at the moment. To hell with Brown.

Keats's brother George's wife, Georgiana Augusta Wylie Keats, has captivated me, and apparently not just me, but Keats as well. Can you imagine, your own brother's wife? And then to watch her sail away, putting an ocean between them (putting Keats and Georgie in pretty much the same situation I am in with Akemi, or *not* in, which is more to the point. But you see, she didn't—sail away, that is. That damned ship sat there on the Mersey for a little over two weeks before there was a breath of air to fill its sails. And Keats had no idea at all. He was too busy walking through Scotland with his dear Brown. But once again, to hell with Brown. I don't like him much.

There is more yet, much more, to both my dissertation and my love life. In fact, this is the heart of it all, what you might call my dilemma. The two are unraveling. Or rather, *raveling*—together. At times I cannot tell where one starts and the other leaves off.

◆

"I don't see you in here with the lady anymore."

The head bartender at The Grille makes this observation after placing the Bloody Mary before me. That was part of the *more* I was trying to tell you about. He is referring to Julia, my former fiancé of one year, who I found sleeping with her boss, Aaron, who in turn will soon be the most powerful legislator in the state of Illinois. They sneaked into that last chapter of my dissertation you just read, in case you hadn't noticed— right into the cabin next to George and Georgiana. There was never any couple by those names booked on The *Telegraph*, American or otherwise.

"No," I say. "We're not together anymore."

"That's too bad," he says without looking up at me, his hands moving so fast to fill drink orders, lifting crystal glasses, picking fruit garnishes, tilting liquor bottles, that he blurs the twenty-something waitress behind him, as if she is in the process of materializing—long legs in black jeans, black beatnik bangs, or as if she is not there at all, simply a mirage. This is not the first time she has caught my eye, only the first time I've let my eye stray long enough to catalogue these details. I try to stop myself. What's wrong with me? Isn't my life complicated enough?

"No, it's all right," I tell the bartender. "It's all for the best this way."

I think the waitress looks at me and smiles faintly as I say this. I turn away as if I have not noticed.

"It often is, pal," the bartender says. "Believe me."

◆

In Ambleside Keats and Brown had nary a chance to indulge in the volumes of Dante and Milton they had packed. The place was a hotbed of political rancor. Certainly the young poet must have been struck by the inequities of the parties involved in the coming election. Only landholders were allowed to vote, and most of them were Tories, political conservatives out to protect the status quo.

And as he hiked along the waterfall, the beauty of which was emblazoned upon his memory if not his soul, Keats's thoughts returned to his brother George, whom he supposed would leave the inn soon to begin his transatlantic trek. In fact, that afternoon he wrote a letter to both George and Georgiana. He and Brown had looked forward to visiting Wordsworth at his home, but were sorry to find the place empty, its famous resident out campaigning for the Tory candidate.

Naturally Keats supported the opposition leader. This was not the first nor the last time Wordsworth would disappoint him, and so as he left Rydal and walked with his companion through Grasmere, consider what an entanglement of sentiments his heart might have generated—

dissatisfaction for the elder man of letters, a certain suspicion of what literary success and a government appointment might do to one's sense of ethics and care for humanity, an ambiguous attraction for his new sister-in-law, conflicted devotion to his own brother.

And now, ensconced in his cabin aboard The Telegraph, *George must have silently considered his own isolation, regardless of the company of Georgiana. Her misgivings were made vocal, defiant as a Jolly Roger— cut off as she was from family, but George could not indulge in the luxury of expressing his own trepidation, must instead remain silent, resolute. Given his brother Tom's worsening physical condition, suffering the latter stages of consumption, he knew they would never again cast eyes upon one another, not in this life. And who could say if he would ever see his sister Fanny again, or his older brother and benefactor John, for that matter? For fifteen days the ship sat upon the murky waters of the Mersey, awaiting even a trace of wind to swell the topsail. And though he and his bride had stayed another five days longer at the Crown Inn than had John and Charles, still—fifteen days! And nothing to stave off his private doubts and loneliness. It must have felt as though he were stuck in a river of time, on a voyage that had no beginning, no end. Every morning he must have checked his Blackberry for some email from Akemi, beautiful Akemi, who had first uplifted his heart and then torn it to shreds, like a Japanese lantern. At times like these, he would softly get up from bed, leave the room and the sleeping Georgie, the petite girl with the black bangs whose timeless eyes were like an enchanting still life of sea waves. Often at midnight he would catch chance glimpses of Julia, the American from the cabin next door, strolling aimlessly on the deck of the ship in the moonlit mist, more a beautiful phantasm than an actual person.*

Well, that's just great. Now I've got Aaron, Julia, Akemi, and the bartending girl all in the nineteenth century during chapter two of my dissertation. And George Keats is back there now on The *Telegraph* trying to get an Internet message from a Japanese woman who will not be born for another 162 years. What do you want from me? I barely sleep. I'm trying to quit smoking. Every woman I fall in love with either runs off with her boss or flies overseas to her husband. And yesterday was my thirty-first birthday, I realized while I was brushing my teeth, and no one sent me so much as a card. Maybe if I spent more time in the real world. But which world is more real?

Look at it this way. It's easy to delete words from a computer. But the real people who insist on remaining real even when I enter my world of Keats . . .if only I could delete *them*. I hadn't expected to find Aaron at her place that night. Or had I? Are not some of our discoveries in fact attempts at verifying what we already suspect? I used to watch them play tennis together, and now I am forced by the sheer robustness of my own imagination to envision what their sporting in bed must have been like.

That's just perverse. *Get your material together, Tom. Think about Keats. Think about Brown. Think about Scotland.*

I don't give a damn about Brown or Scotland.

No back talk, now. Concentrate on the details. Look through your notes, anything that sheds light on the direction of Keats's thoughts and desires, the development of his soul. Come on, now.

Christ—all this Keats information, minutiae, notes scribbled on candy bar wrappers, receipts. What do I do with it all?

Okay, so he had syphilis, Keats did, and almost canceled the walking trip. Caught it at Oxford, the bawdy little brat. At least that's what is hinted at in some of the biographical material. I guess that might be enough to make him resent women. He was "taking Mercury"—and the only thing anyone took mercury for was syphilis, and of course the only thing mercury would do is poison you, hasten dementia, and that was one condition Keats did not have to worry about. He'd be dead soon enough. Brown would not have included any mention of venereal disease in his later memoirs, which were so deferential. Of course, I had better check that. As you know I have my own questions about Brown. He was not just inordinately affectionate; he even describes Keats's "sensual" mouth. If he was in love with him, fine, but let's just get it out on the goddamn table.

Let's see, Brown was thirty-one during the walk, Keats twenty-two. But here's another point of contention, another matter that requires factual verification—one source puts Georgiana's age at sixteen, but

I just came across another that says she was twenty-one. A five year discrepancy among so-called experts! What kind of experts are these? And who gets involved with a teenager before crossing the ocean, other than Roman Polanski?

Where is this thing going, this dissertation? It reads like a pretzeled third person narrative, and I have not been granted that kind of uncommon creative freedom by my committee. Now I tumble headlong into it, find my own life within the lines.

Just one cigarette, I promise myself, and then I'll quit again tomorrow. What did I do with my matches?

◆

The fall term will begin in a few weeks. The sunsets are all orange and veer south at the end of day. I have finished my work and come early to The Grille. The svelte girl in black is tending bar alone. She places a Bloody Mary in front of me and wipes the counter with a rag.

"Ed, the head bartender, told me you're not with the lady anymore. I used to see you guys in here all the time." I take a sip of the drink and look up at her as a reply. There is an awkward moment, big as a stalled ship on a northern British river. "I don't mean to pry."

Sure you do, I think. *Go ahead and pry.*

"She was in here the other day," she says. "She left this for you."

The girl with the bangs hands me a stiff envelope—obviously a greeting card—with just my name written upon it, the exaggerated flourishes typical of Julia's handwriting.

Thomas O'Connell

Julia never called me *Thomas* in her life. Under the rhymed Hallmark happy birthday inanities is the inscription: *Fondly, Julia.* It makes me feel as though an aunt had just made a kissing sound near one of my ears. And why bring it here instead of mail it? She must have been certain that I would be drinking rather than working. Well, she had always known me, more or less.

"I found her sleeping with her boss," I say.

96

"Oh, my God."

Julia. At odd moments I find my thoughts returning to her out of habit, the way the image of a house you used to live in appears before you now and then, unbidden.

"But it's okay, because I was losing interest in her. I'd fallen for another woman, a Japanese woman. But she got called back overseas."

She arranges a stainless steel bin filled with lemon slices distractedly, looks away, thoughtful.

"Then I found out she had a husband. She let it slip in an email."

Now she has stopped and looks directly at me, the corners of her mouth up-turned slightly. "The old slip of the email. You really ought to learn to open up a little, quit trying to hold everything in."

The Bloody Mary is a work of art. And I didn't expect the repartee. Can't be older than what—twenty-five? She goes to wait on another customer while I feign interest in a baseball game on the flat screen television over the bar, the green field, the yellow padding of the catcher's mask. I do not even know which teams are playing. When everybody cheers, I cheer too.

A-ke-mi Mo-ri-o-ka. Her name whispers through my thoughts like a secret wish. I recall the simple elegance of the words in her essays, like unexpected strings of aural pearls. It was through them that I fell in love with her spirit. For what are words other than the pure projection of our souls?

Lucky Keats. He's dead in Italy. All the women who vexed or entranced him are dead too, either in England or America. But Akemi is very much alive and in Tokyo. With her husband.

And so the question that spins in the hamster wheel of my brain is, *How could she have a husband?* Translate: *How could she have a husband who is not me?* Nobody filled me in before I fell in love with her. I just walked around under the assumption that there was a chance that the most beautiful, gentle, graceful woman in the world might consider the possibility of marrying me, in which case *I* would be her husband, the way the universe, fate—God, for Christ's sake—had intended me to be. Who is this man, this husband, and where did he come from?

I know where he came from—Japan. But what I mean is, how

could he have beat me to it, to *her*? Well, he knew her first—which strikes me as nothing more than an unfair advantage. There is no way out of this. The hamster is on the wheel and he won't get off, and so I sit and stare at the bar and I think. I think of Akemi Morioka.

The girl in black returns with another freshly made Bloody Mary, sets it down hard on the wooden surface before me. "I figured you were going to need this," she says.

Two out at the bottom of the first inning. I still do not know who is playing.

"You sure come in here a lot. What do you do?" she asks.

"I'm an English professor. Well, part time, actually. I'm doing research, trying to finish my dissertation."

"Really? My favorite book in high school was *The Great Gatsby.*"

She tells me this as she serves two other customers, her hands in a frenetic ballet between liquor bottles and draft beer pulls. That slightly upturned nose, the hazel eyes framed by the anachronistic bangs. I tell her that the house in which F. Scott Fitzgerald's first love lived is a scant five blocks away.

"Really?" She beams.

"I'll take you for a walk past it, if you like. When do you get off?"

The question makes her smile coyly. She washes a glass in the stainless steel sink behind the bar and looks far away.

◆

"Her name was Genevra King," I say, as we stroll in the carroty glow of the Lake Forest sunset, light filtered through green, leafy boughs. Ornate streetlamps begin to glow as I trace the outline of the home with my extended forefinger. "She lived right there."

"Is she the one he wrote the book about?"

"No—it's hard to tell. His wife, Zelda came into his life not long after she spoke that famous line to him, the one about rich girls not marrying poor boys. I think he wrote a short story about her, though."

"What's it called?"

I stop in front of the house. She is a slender, pretty girl. She radiates the freshness and energy of youth. I wonder where this is going, and whether it is an indication of how truly lonely I am.

"'Winter Dreams.' The girl's name in the story is Judy Jones. She's wealthy and beautiful, and he falls in love with her when she's only eleven, and then she comes and goes into his life for years afterward, breaking his heart each time—until finally she loses her beauty, and he weeps for the end of it, the beauty, that is."

She pulls a leaf from a branch that dawdles above us in the evening breeze. I feel young and irresponsible, as if I am on my first date—ever. We turn the corner around King's home, beneath blankets of greenery in the treetops, and she appears so urbane, enigmatic.

And then she says, "Would you like me to channel her?"

The evening crashes to a halt. You can hear safety glass tinkling.

"Pardon?"

"Genevra King. Would you like me to channel her?"

The leaf twirls between her fingers, brushes against her lips.

"What do you mean—*channel* her?"

She rolls her eyes and continues down the sidewalk. Darkness gathers in the eastern sky. "*You* know, get in touch with her spirit and all, *become* her, for a while."

I look at her as if she has gone crazy.

"It's just something I do."

It's just something she does, absorbing dead people's spirits. Oh, well. And now I see the value of online dating services. They can screen out the channelers.

"No, thanks," I say. Then I stop, just past the hedges of the white mansion. "Why would you offer to channel Genevra King?"

"To help you with your dissertation about Fitzgerald."

"But I'm not writing about Fitzgerald. I'm writing about Keats."

She shrugs, says she doesn't know anything about Keats. She can't channel men. Then she asks if I would like to come up to her apartment.

Can you even imagine how lonely I am?

I am sprawled upon a pillow in the bed of the young bartender.

I think for a moment of Keats's attraction to his sister-in-law, how he might have blamed women in general for the desire he felt toward them. And this girl in bed with me—skin as smooth as polished marble, eyes mysterious and alluring. Behind them lie chambers mysterious, unfathomable. I look around her room, taped posters of rock groups on the walls. THE ALTAR BOYS. MILLIONS OF DEAD COPS. GET DEAD. I recall nights with Julia, how the conversation would always turn to politics, or acquiring property in a fashionable neighborhood. I'll bet Julia doesn't know a thing about The Altar Boys.

She reaches to the night stand, two-fingers a Camel Light from a crumpled package, and lights it. From beneath the edge of the bed sheet, which is nearly the same tone as her flesh, I spy for the first time a tattoo of a skull and crossbones on her thigh.

"Can you really do it?" I say.

She releases a jet of gray-blue smoke toward the ceiling, shapes the ash of her cigarette on the inside of a Mike's Hard Lemonade bottle. "Didn't I just?"

"No—I mean channeling."

She smiles as she wraps the sheet around her small, tight breasts and reaches out to touch me. "Who would you like me to channel?"

"Her name was Georgie—Georgiana Augusta Wylie."

The cigarette end sizzles in the bottle. Placing it carefully on the nightstand, she reclines upon two stacked pillows and closes her eyes.

"I'll have to know something about her—a time, a place."

I sit up, hover over her. "She was born in seventeen-ninety-eight. In eighteen-eighteen she sailed from Liverpool to Philadelphia, with her new husband. There is reason to believe—"

Now, is this just conjecture on my part? Wishful thinking?

"Yes?" she says, ever so faintly.

"There is reason to believe she regretted marrying him. They sailed on a ship called The *Telegraph*."

She breathes deeply and exhales slowly, once, twice. All is still, quiet. She is framed in a halo of twilight moonbeam, skin so flawless and milky, as if painted upon a vase.

From deep down inside comes a languorous, whispered query.

"Tell me my name. Tell me who I am."

"Georgie," I say in a hush. "Georgie Augusta Wylie."

Her lips move, but there is no sound.

I reflect for a moment on what we have experienced together tonight. I don't know if in fact beauty is truth, and vice versa, but I know she is beautiful. It's like falling from a mountainside, or allowing myself to fall from one, this plunging into another's soul all the time, first Julia, then Akemi, and now—*Georgie*.

◆

Awakening each fresh day, still motionless upon the Mersey, the walls of the ship's cabin closing in upon her, her original suspicion crystallized—that she had acted precipitously in submitting to sojourn across the ocean, and in agreeing to marry this man in the first place. It was a mistake, a girlish one. Though young, she was not in the least naïve, especially when it came to the effect she had upon men, certain men, how she could capture and hold their attention without meaning to, the way she had with her husband's brother, John.

And even after the vessel had begun to sail into the open sea like a great creature free of a trap, she felt herself more stultified by her circumstances, the close quarters with a husband she was not in love with. How could she be—after what he had done to his own family member? There was something inherently dishonest, greedy in this man—unashamed to beg his brother John for his own rightful portion of the inheritance. It was clear he was already living hand-to-mouth, and now with the decision to give up his career in medicine for the hare-brained scheme of becoming a scribbler of verse—he was likely to end up on the dole, a beggar, kept warm in some charity house, or by the waning embers of some church's poor hearth.

By the time the couple reached port in the new country, she was desperate to seize the moment, to declare her intention to flee the dual prisons of her marriage and her intimate proximity to this man. But the moment never quite presented itself. Where would she go? To whom could she cleave? The letter had not made the decision easier for her, the one that was awaiting them in Philadelphia, from Keats. In a fit of affection he had written a silly acrostic poem for her, based on the beginning letters of her name—GEORGIANA AUGUSTA KEATS.

> *Anthropophagi in Othello's mood,*
> *Ulysses stormed, and his enchanted belt*
> *Glow with the muse, but they are never felt*
> *Unbosom'd so and so eternal made,*
> *Such tender incense in their laurel shade,*
> *To all the regent sisters of the Nine,*
> *As this poor offering to you, sister mine.*

She let the pages fall from her hand to her lap. This was not even bad poetry—it was worse. Poor John. He should have been setting bones.

George wandered about, dragging them to New York, Pittsburgh, without a plan. He was hoodwinked out of the little money he had left, and finally, by the time they had reached Cincinnati, worn, tired and dirty, they were destitute, and whatever fire of passion there might once have been between them was extinguished.

But Georgie was a survivor. She took a job as a barkeep at Cincinnati's finest tavern, and caused a minor sensation with her own concoction made from tomato juice, Tabasco, horseradish, and vodka. Patrons flocked, and soon she was a part owner.

George, humiliated by her success, sailed back to England and bent his older brother's metaphorical arm for more of the inheritance, including his brother Tom's—for Tom did not live to see the approaching holiday season. He said he had already purchased land and needed the funds immediately, when in fact he was only planning to make the purchase.

This was too much for the girl. In her husband's absence she made the acquaintance of a handsome, up and coming writer, Thomas O'Connell, who shot to fame and fortune soon thereafter with his great American novel, Forgetting Julia and Akemi. *Georgie was granted a divorce from George, and she and O'Connell married and made millions of dollars from book royalties and marketing her recipe for a new drink she dubbed the Bloody Mary, after Queen Mary I. She sold the rights to*

Fernand Petiot, of New York.

Poor John Keats died, relatively unknown.

George returned from England, fathered eight children in Louisville, and died of (what else?) consumption.

Oh, and O'Connell was no longer answerable to an English department committee because no one knew who the hell Keats was. This alleviated a growing difficulty he'd had with distinguishing reality from fantasy.

And so they lived, happily, on what seemed to them a river of time.

Where People Go

Dad died the spring I turned eleven. I remember how green the grass was, how blue the sky. Massive heart attack, they said. Mom found him in his study, slumped over a volume of Wordsworth, his favorite poet. The text was open to page 293—"Composed upon Westminster Bridge":

> *Earth hath not anything to show more fair:*
> *Dull would he be of soul who could pass by*
> *A sight so touching in its majesty:*
> *This City now doth, like a garment, wear*
> *The beauty of the morning; silent, bare,*

Because it was the last thing he read, I made it my business to know the poem well, to memorize it. Neither was I any stranger to its subject matter, delight at the accidental and thoroughly unexpected discovery of natural beauty.

I suppose every boy believes his father to be the greatest man in the world, and I was no different. I'll even go so far as to say that he may well have *been* the greatest man in the world, which made it all the more difficult. We had never been separated from one another, and I can't remember having left the house without first a touch or a word from him. Oh, we were tight. Worse even than his death was the irreversible fact that I hadn't been given a chance to say good-bye.

Now it was autumn again and I was back in school, the sixth grade, I believe. Yes, it was the sixth grade. I know, because in my memory glass Mrs. Bodhesten appears in front of the class at the chalkboard, wan and ill-tempered, as some older teachers can be. She was speaking that afternoon, that glorious, Indian summer afternoon, of *manufacturing*. It was a word I'd been hearing a lot of lately. I had no idea what it meant. It sounded foreign and significant and incomprehensible. The clock, the one that often seemed to come to a complete halt for hours on end, had just hit the pivotal five-to-three mark and refused to budge any farther. Mrs. Bodhesten's voice faded away as time froze and my world fell out of orbit. The queasy sensation in my chest expanded until I thought it might swallow me up, a feeling I recognize today as the physical component that accompanies loss, in this case, the loss of my father. When it struck (and it struck often back then, several times a day), I reached in my back pocket for the remedy I used to treat it—a letter Dad had written to me the previous year. Dad liked to write me letters. He was a professor of literature. For him it was easier to write his feelings down than to simply talk about them. Or perhaps that's not true. It may just be, and I have a pretty certain inkling that I'm onto something here, but it just may be that he didn't believe that the expression of his feelings was *valid* unless it was first committed to the written word. I still have that letter, on my person, in fact, and at all times. Like me, it has seen crisper, more legible days, and fewer creases.

Dear Jonah:

I was thinking about what you'd told me over dinner. The way I get it, you're angry at yourself for having missed the baseball team tryouts, and maybe you're feeling a little sorry for yourself as well. I understand your predicament. I think it would throw me for a loop if I were in your shoes, too. But let's see if I can't put it into some kind of perspective for you, pull a silver lining out of my hat.

If you had made it to the team audition, you would have been judged not by your level of enthusiasm, but by your level of ability, and if I recall correctly, you were aiming for the lofty center stage role of pitcher, which is admirable, very gutsy. I happen to know that you are a competent, even an *impressive* center-fielder. You can snag flies and pick off runaway grounders like nobody's business. However, I have also seen you pitch, and to be ruthlessly frank, which is a father's privilege and sometimes even his obligation, your curve needs work, and you haven't got a fast ball. In all probability, you would not have been the best pitching prospect out there, or the second best, either, in which case you've saved yourself considerable embarrassment. If you want to rue the loss of the center field position—well then, that you *almost* have the right to do, because you would've been the best candidate. But you weren't interested in being a center-fielder, and you wouldn't have tried out for the position anyway, so nothing lost. Also, remember why you missed the audition in the first place—to go to Spider's birthday party. To you it might not have seemed like such an earth-stopping experience, but to her it meant everything, and I'm sure she'll never forget it. Good for you.

Do I think you can be a pitcher someday? Absolutely. It's unanimous—you and me both. But before that can happen, there is a thing called *work* that you have to attend to, and you'll need lots of it before you are ready to be a pitcher. Success is all about timing, Jonah. When you sense the time is right, when you know it in your heart, that's when you make your move. And don't be disappointed, don't kick yourself if you miss an opportunity, just as you've missed the team tryouts. You'll be surprised throughout your life how missed opportunities have a way of re-presenting themselves. Just don't miss them the second time around.

"Mr. Wander?"

Time abruptly jolted back into gear and I was looking up into the prunish face of Mrs. Bodhesten. She had asked me something, but I had been in another world.

I said, "Huh?"

"*Huh* is not an answer. I asked you if you could tell me about the chief goods manufactured in the northeastern United States."

I blinked involuntarily and looked at my father's letter, then at her. "No."

"No *what*?"

"No, Mrs. Bodhesten."

My face burned as I heard giggles erupt in the back of the room. It always amazed me what traitors classmates could be if given a fraction of a chance. They loved nothing better than to see one of their own catch it and catch it big.

Mrs. Bodhesten walked slowly down the aisle between the wooden school desks until she reached me.

"Mr. Wander's mind seems to be wandering." I looked sheepishly up at her as the class burst into ringing, raucous laughter—not the sweet laughter children are capable of, but the other, darker kind. I was held suspended by distress over how big the pores in Mrs. Bodhesten's nose were. "I would say that *Wander* is an appropriate name for you, wouldn't you, Jonah?"

As big as buttons they were. "Yes, Mrs. Bodhesten."

Looking dispassionately into my eyes, she removed my father's letter from my fingers and snatched it up.

"Notes?"

"No," I said, standing, reaching desperately for the letter, *my* letter. She raised it over her head, where I could not reach it. The bell rang.

"Mr. Wander will remain in his seat. The rest of you may leave—*and don't forget your reports on manufacturing for tomorrow!*"

The school room took on a ghostly and unfamiliar look as it emptied. Small noises, like the hinges on my desk top, echoed. My heart pounded against my ribs as I watched Mrs. Bodhesten read the letter at her desk. She dropped it on her blotter when she had finished and eyed me disparagingly. I could actually hear the thin electric buzz of the clock as the red second hand rounded its way past the two, the three. Outside the bright autumn sunshine warmed the breeze that found its way in through the classroom windows, rotary windows that cranked noisily and stubbornly open. The shrill sound of young voices rose and fell and drifted off.

"And who is it that writes nonsense about baseball and makes excuses for your indolence?"

I didn't understand. "My *what*?"

"*In-do-lence*," she said, breaking the word into syllables for my benefit. "Your failure to appear at the baseball auditions."

"Oh. That was my father."

Bzzzzzzz. The clock. Mrs. Bodhesten screwed up her face (a lot of screwing) and folded her hands deliberately and authoritatively before her. Her nails were dull yellow and had been cut to the nub. "I should think he would have had more sense than to suggest excuses to an impressionable boy."

"My father," I said, breathing rapid, shallow breaths, "had a *lot* of sense."

She unfolded her hands, flipped the letter over on her desk, and said, "I sympathize with your loss, Jonah Wander. But I will not permit daydreaming or personal notes in my class. You are dismissed."

I stood up and placed a notebook in my school bag. I walked slowly to the front of the room, down squared borders of linoleum tile that seemed to telescope out in front of me, two for every one I crossed. When I dared to look up, the harsh glare of fluorescent light tubes reflected off the metal rims of Mrs. Bodhesten's glasses.

"I said, you are dismissed, boy,"

My letter. I couldn't leave without my letter. Slowly, deliberately, as if gifted with the knowledge of what I was thinking, she folded it up along the creases and slipped it inside her desk drawer, which she then locked with a key. I wanted to say something, but my jaw quivered so that I was unable to form words.

"You can get your note back when your mother comes in for a conference with me. Any day after school is fine, but Tuesdays and Thursdays are better."

The quivering had spread from my jaw to my legs. If I could

turn back the clock and appear in front of her now as an adult, I suspect my voice would fail me all over again.

"Go!" she commanded, and at the crack of that word as it ricocheted off the cinder-block walls, I launched like a rocket out of the room and down the hall, never stopping until I found myself in the sanctuary of the school yard, next to the bicycle rack, a pool of leaves spinning in dizzying circles near my ankles.

"What'd she do to you?"

It was Spider. Spider was my best friend, even though she was a girl. You might not have known she was a girl at first glance. She wore overalls and sneakers and could climb a tree better than most boys I knew. Still, we never played together at school—only afterward. If anyone would have known about us, they would have made our lives an obstacle course of taunts.

"Nothing," I said, pulling my bike out of the rack and jumping on the seat.

"Wait!" Spider called out behind me. "Wanna stop by Saletra's and buy some football cards?"

"Can't," I shouted over my shoulder, riding like the wind down the black-topped drive of the school onto Orchard Street, beneath the golden, leaf-heavy boughs of shade trees. I didn't once look back.

The October afternoon was thick with mist and smoke as I sped down the streets of old Lake Forest, in Illinois. The embers of burning leaves created an incense that aimed at the heart. The sky was a bluish haze, and to the experienced bicycle rider, every foot of sidewalk, each bump and fissure was a landmark that pointed the way home. But I wasn't headed home. With an easy nudge of the handlebar grips I veered onto Western Avenue, where wildflowers grew among the weeds near the railroad tracks. I stopped there and flicked my kick stand. On my hands and knees I pulled out a bouquet of purple and yellow blossoms, discarding the occasional tall prairie grass that got mixed in.

Back on my bike, I traveled a dirt road to the very edge of town, past ancient houses whose lowered patio umbrellas lent no illusions about the season at hand, as if mourning forgotten summer afternoons. Squirrels swept lawns on their bellies for acorns. I recall the dominance of withered willow trees dangling victoriously over their skeletal neighbors, ash and elms and maples. My bicycle cut through waist-high overgrowth. In the distance came the wavering sound of chain saws, and on some afternoons, the more ominous *cha-pops* of hunters' rifles, deep in the woods to the west.

Just at the edge of what used to be thicket, a tame and serene expanse of lawn opened up, the old Ridgewood Cemetery. I guided my bike onto the narrow drive and knew when I was nearing my father's place, because of a neat, diagonal row of shagbark trees. I lowered the bike to the soft ground and walked to his marker.

Jonathan Charles Wander
1930-1972

Each time I read it I felt queasy, the gravestone confirming for real what I had been attempting to convince myself was only a bad dream, a wild invention of the imagination. My father was dead.

I laid the flowers upon the marker and then sat, my legs folded beneath me. I patted the ground above him, stroking the blades of grass, recollecting the way his sweaters felt, the soft, warm wool that smelled of pipe smoke, a good friendly smell, Dad's smell.

"I read a letter of yours today," I said. "You left it on my dresser one night and I found it the next morning. Do you remember?"

Yes—I spoke to him, but only when I was certain I was alone. If someone happened to walk past, I would pretend I was praying, and when they were gone, I would begin again.

"My teacher caught me reading it during social studies and took it away. I'll get it back, though. Don't worry. Mom has to come to school. She's going to be mad, 'cause she'll have to miss work." I carefully arranged the wildflowers together, so they were all even along the tops. "Mom's not doing so hot. She has to work now, at a bank. When she gets home she's tired. We hardly ever have dinner together, like we used to. You know those lines she gets on her forehead when she's worried about stuff? Right here—" I pointed to my own forehead, drew an imaginary groove with my finger. "She's got those all the time, 'cause she's always reading legal papers about the house and the insurance and all. And she took your pictures down. It's not the same anymore."

Then suddenly, unexpectedly, images surrounded me, indistinct at first, murky, like dream impressions. Dad was sitting in the box seats of Wrigley Field during a Chicago Cubs baseball game, yelling at the umpire, his hands cupped around his mouth, big strong hands. Next I saw him at Lake Geneva, casting a line from the shore, reeling it in ever so slowly, standing tall beside the water's edge, his reflection shimmering upon the surface. And then he was picking me up from my first big spill on a two-wheeler, his arms comforting, his chest solid. He looked so *real*, so alive. It seemed as though I could reach out and touch him, but the impressions soon faded; all that was left before me was empty air, the startling blue of the sky, and strangely, the premature moon hanging silvery overhead. I lay down on the grassy mound and buried my face in my arms. When a hand touched me from behind, I think I may have jumped a mile.

"Jonah?"

It was Spider. She had followed me.

"What're you doing?" I said. I was on my feet in a sliver of an instant, wiping my eyes dry, frightened nearly out of my senses.

"Shh," Spider said, holding a finger to her lips. "This is a *cemetery.*"

"I know what it is," I said. "What do you think I'm going to do— wake them all up? They're never waking up again." I sat down beside my bike, my back to Spider, and began methodically pulling blades of grass out of the ground.

"I didn't mean to scare you."

"You didn't scare me," I lied.

She stood directly behind me now. I studied the grass intently.

"Did you get in trouble with Bodhesten? What's she going to do to you?"

"My mom's got to come to school."

"Who was the note from?"

I tilted my head toward the grave.

"From your *father*?"

111

I nodded.

Spider sat down next to me. "She shouldn't have done that."

I didn't say anything.

"She had no right."

I stuck a prairie weed in the corner of my mouth. "What's *manufacturing*?" I said.

"Huh?"

"That word she's always using. What does it mean?"

Spider shook her head. "You've been daydreaming, you."

"I can't help it. She's so damn boring all the time."

"You shouldn't swear in a cemetery. It's bad luck."

"I don't care."

"Don't you ever pay attention in class?"

"Sometimes," I said. "I paid attention when she read that poem by Robert Forest—'Stopping by Woods on a Snowy Evening.'"

"His name is *Frost*. Robert *Frost*, not *Forest*."

"Still, it's a pretty good poem. Even *she* can't ruin it."

Then Spider did something funny, something I didn't expect. She put her arm around my shoulder. "Anyway," she said, "you don't got to cry."

"I wasn't crying."

She didn't buy it. You couldn't fool Spider. "Your father's in heaven now. He's real happy."

"How do you know?"

"'Cause everybody's happy in heaven."

"No, I mean, how do you know he's there?"

"You don't think he's in the other place, do you?"

"Of course not. But how do you know there's a heaven?"

"Jonah Wander, don't you know *anything*? Where do you think people go when they . . . when they—"

We both sat quietly for a while without looking at each other. A little breeze started up and flattened a section of grass as though it had been brushed by an invisible hand.

"It means making things, like in a factory," Spider said at last.

"What does?"

"*Manufacturing.*"

So *that's* what it meant. Such a big word for something so ordinary, so unimportant.

"I miss him, Spider."

She sat down in front of me and stared at me hard, dead on, her pixie bangs dancing in the wind. She rolled up the cuffs of her overalls to just beneath her knees, exposing the white skin of her shins. "I know you do, Jonah. I know you miss him, but you can't keep doing this."

I squinted at her doubtfully. "Doing what?"

Spider sighed and rolled her eyes at the sky. "Don't you think I know that you come here every day after school, sometimes even *before* school?" Those were supposed to have been our times, my father and me, but she knew my secret, had followed me. I didn't know whether to feel surprised or betrayed, though I was aware that my father had always been partial to Spider, and that spoke volumes on her behalf. Still, it was a sneaky thing to have done. Then she said this: "You're not the same anymore, Jonah, and you won't ever be, unless you say good-bye to him."

"Unless I *what*?"

At this she shook her head. "I swear I never saw a boy like you before. You don't listen to a thing anybody says."

"Just tell me what I got to do again."

"I said, you got to say *good-bye* to your father. Sooner or later you do, anyways."

It was like a thunderbolt, hearing her say that, the notion that it wasn't too late to make my peace with Dad. I hadn't ever considered that, hadn't been thinking about this clearly or correctly at all. It called to mind some very sage advice I'd been reading a lot of lately:

You'll be surprised throughout your life how missed opportunities have a way of re-presenting themselves. Just don't miss them the second time around.

Spider stood up and walked over to her bicycle. There were freckles on the backs her ankles, myriad little brown blotches. I don't know why, but I was very happy and relieved to see them. She tilted her head for me to follow and took my hand. I felt something surprising, extraordinary in the touch of her fingers upon my palm. I got up and followed her.

Till Death Do us Part

Gwen and I hate each other. It was not always like this. When I first saw her, leaning over a forty-foot Beneteau sailboat, struggling with a mooring rope in Diversey Harbor, my heart rose to my throat. Such beauty! Cream white complexion, rounded cheeks, blasé eyes so unselfconscious as to appear skylights to her soul, before I discovered she didn't have one. All of which prompted me to call out from the pier, "Ahoy there, sailor. Need a hand?"

It was her father's rig, the boat. He was a former Navy man who did not much appreciate a landlubber trying to pick up his daughter. That was shortly before his bankruptcy—an event that started off slowly and then picked up speed, like a Yankee Clipper. It might have had something to do with her decision to jump ship and marry me, the bankruptcy. As a matter of fact, I 'm pretty sure it had a *lot* to do with it. We have been married the better part of fourteen years, and as I say, now we hate one another. Like her father's bankruptcy proceedings, it happened slowly at first. A late night at the office and I came home to Attila the Hun—stressed out from being cooped up in the house all day with a crying, pooping spit-up machine that passed as a child. There was wild fire in Gwen's eyes that I had never seen before. Hair disheveled, bathrobe askew, she was stuffing a soiled diaper in the garbage next to a Gerber Pea Puree baby food jar when I said, "Hi, honey. I'm home."

What would *you* have expected? A kiss? A kind word? And what would you have thought when a Similac formula can was hurled within an inch of your head, cracking against the newly painted wall of your kitchen, knocking plaster dust on your navy blue Kenneth Cole suit? Would you have thought, *Well, it's just a phase. She's a little testy from the demands of child rearing—*?

That's what I thought. But the phase grew in duration and intensity until it became a way of life. Soon there were fights that made Normandy look like a school-yard scrap. Gwen's aim improved. Cans and pans no longer dented plaster. Now they pummeled *me*, with dead-eye accuracy. And talk about obscenities—she had the mouth of a sailor. It was genetic.

The only peace I knew was when I escaped for a few hours (usually just a jump or a skip ahead of a flying utensil) to the links. I golf. I love golf. I love golf the way I used to love my wife. Put me on a fairway and my heart rises to my throat at the sight of the smooth complexion of the turf, the rounded curves of sand traps. The course is redolent of nature's sweet scents. Endless miles of perfectly groomed landscape call out to me, "You're home, honey. Take out your putter." And when I mentally replay our latest skirmish, I grasp the shaft of my driver and transfer all my righteous indignation to the little white Titleist balanced upon the tee, whacking it up, up into the air, until it disappears in the distance and sails gently back to earth. Life *can* be good.

It was in 2008, I think, when I knew we were in real trouble. I'm in advertising. I had just come home from a late dinner presentation to a client who as much as told me that I did not understand his product and that my ideas were stupid. I walked in the front door and ducked, expecting to be greeted by something airborne—a pot, an iron, a Scud missile, when instead I found Gwen reading "Hansel and Gretel" to our boys. It was a Rockwell scene.

"Don't you look gruesome," Gwen said to me, my boy Arnold on her lap. My younger son, Palmer, was curled at her feet, untying her shoelaces.

"The account exec at Sawyer just trashed my presentation," I told her. "I had the whole project outlined. I'd worked on it for weeks."

"But you're an idiot," she said, cuddling the children around her like Lady Madonna.

"Gwen, don't say that in front of the boys."

"Daddy's a big, big idiot," she sing-sang to Arnold.

Little Palmer looked up from her shoe and said, "Daddy's a big fat slob."

"And where did he learn that, as if I have to ask?"

Gwen giggled and patted Palmer's head. "From Mommy. Because it's *true,* isn't it, Palmer? Daddy's a big, big—"

"—son-of-a-bish!" he finished for her, his little round face convulsed in innocent glee.

It was a Rockwell scene, all right—a *George Lincoln* Rockwell scene.

Hatred tore at my heart, boiled in my recently acquired ulcer, festered within my bowels. "Gwen?" I said with restraint, setting my briefcase on the floor. "May I see you in the kitchen?"

"What's Daddy? Hm? What's Daddy again?"

"Son-of-a-bish! *Fat* son-of-a-bish!"

"Gwen? Now, please."

"I'll get up when I'm ready."

I bit my tongue, left the room, and body-slammed the swinging kitchen door. Breath came in hot anxious gulps. I poured myself three fingers of Glenfiddich and chugged it. The liquid fire in my throat fortified me. When Gwen sashayed into the kitchen, her arrogant head tilted up as if she had a hard-boiled egg balanced on her chin, I squeezed my highball glass so that it broke, cutting a deep meaty gash in the palm of my hand. Blood poured down my wrist, stained my Ralph Lauren shirt, and glopped onto the tiled floor like so much ketchup. Strangely, it bothered me not at all. In fact, I enjoyed it. It spurred me on. I remember the look of alarm on Gwen's face, the distorted twist of her lips as she regarded my wound, the flinch of her eyes as I allowed what was left of the glass to smash to the floor, where it rained tiny shards. For a brief moment I half-expected her to utter a fearful word of concern, to show some kind solicitude over my ripped flesh.

"You imbecile. You can't even hold a glass properly."

This woman was a miracle of science: she was alive, but she had no heart.

Abruptly, I swung at her, calculating a brutish blow to the temple, but the filaments of civilization caught me up like a spastic marionette and ruined the follow-through. My hand, numbly exsanguinating, spurting like a plasma fountain, froze in midair as she braced for the impact. *What the hell,* I thought, and then gently smeared a bloody streak across her face, a glistening red trail from nose to ear. She recoiled in disgust. The three-quarter heel of her beige Cole Hahn pump came down hard on the soft leather toe of my Domani loafer. She *impaled* me. Then it was tit for tat as I painted the rest of her face and she intermittently kicked, clawed and gouged every unprotected inch of my body. I collapsed against her, embraced her like a boxer enervated, trapped in a corner of the ring. That stopped her cold. Until I slipped. We were Jack and Jill without a hill, just the ruby mosh pit of the tile floor.

Arnold and Palmer pushed open the swinging door and found us like that.

So we put them in therapy.

"Mr. Lipschitz," the balding, dapper child psychologist said to me after the first session, pulling on his Vandyke, "would you care to see a picture little Palmer drew tonight?"

"Not very much, no."

He produced a crayon sketch from a manila folder. Crimson swirls against a white background. "Here it is, anyway. When I asked him what it was supposed to be, he said, 'Daddy—killing Mommy.'"

I swallowed. "I obviously didn't kill her."

"Perhaps to him, you *did.*"

He held the drawing out to me, but I turned away. The stick figure Daddy in the picture was smiling. I doubled over and wept into my open hands.

I had always thought marriage counseling was a crock, for the birds. Dr. Norton Heckler, our counselor, a too-amiable sharpy who looked disarmingly like Regis Philbin's younger brother, did very little to alter my opinion. Every meeting was the same. First he encouraged Gwen to enumerate her complaints against me, and she complied with vertiginous redundancy.

"This isn't a marriage, doctor," she *kvetched,* "it's medieval couples torture. That bastard never spends a second with me or the children—"

"Is that proper? Should she be allowed to call me a bastard?" I protested.

"Allow her to continue, Mr. Lipschitz," Regis's brother said.

"—he's married to his *job*, which he stinks at, by the way."

"That's not fair!"

"Mr. Lipschitz, please."

"We never go out; he never takes me anyplace."

"Of *course* I don't take you anyplace! We can't stand *being* with each other!"

"Mr. Lipschitz, let her finish."

"Why, we've never even had a vacation, not once in fourteen years."

"We can't afford one, Gwen. Why can't you get that through your—"

"But we can afford your goddamn sports car, can't we? Your youth-mobile, you pathetic, fat—"

"It's an investment! I spend a hell of a lot less on my Austin Healey than you do on clothes and jewelry. Ten thousand dollars last year at Neiman Marcus alone!"

Then I was asked to sit out in the waiting room while Heckler spent the rest of the session with Gwen alone. I don't know what went on in there. Occasionally I put my ear to the door, but I heard nothing. By the end of the first month in counseling, I'd sold my Austin Healey and Gwen had returned the clothes from her last shopping binge. We were both miserable and fought more than ever.

"What I think I need to do," Dr. Heckler explained to me earnestly, during a rare one-on-one session, "is spend time with Gwen in your home environment."

"What?"

"To see things from your perspective. Unless I can discover what triggers your anger, Mr. Lipschitz, I'm afraid I can't help you."

"What do you mean, exactly, spend time with Gwen in our home environment?"

119

Dr. Heckler sat on the love seat with Gwen and the children while I hid behind a newspaper on my La-Z-Boy.

"I want to play with my new Daddy," Arnold said.

"Me too!" screeched Palmer.

"Look here," I objected, letting the paper furl to my lap, "aren't you confusing the children? Should they be calling you *Daddy*?"

"We're *role-playing*, Mr. Lipschitz. This is as healthy for them as it is for you and your wife. Now, observe." He turned to Gwen and held her hand in his. "Dear, how was your day?"

Gwen transmuted into Laura Petry before my eyes. "Oh, you know. Errands, the children. How was *your* day, darling?"

"She never calls me darling," I interrupted.

"Well, you never ask me how my day was, you fat bastard."

"Do you see?" I blurted.

Dr. Heckler remained unfazed. He was still in character. "Gwen, would you and the children care to go out for sundaes?"

"I'd love to."

"Yay!" yelled Arnold.

"Yippee!" Palmer joined in.

The four of them rose merrily and hiked it up to the Baskin-Robbins, leaving me home alone to play the role of a fat bastard in his La-Z-Boy.

"You call that a *slogan*?" Sloan Dovedale, copy chief at Hirsch and Bristol, had just shared with me his assessment of my new campaign for Rooty-Tooties, a tart, semi-toxic candy for which eight year olds around the globe seemed to have developed a jones. "'Rooty-Tooties will kick your booty,'" he read aloud. "Three weeks' work, and this is what you hand me. How am I supposed to fly this past the FCC? Do I have to remind you about truth in advertising?"

A sickening suspicion crept like a tarantula through my thoughts: maybe everything *was* my fault. They had all looked so happy together last night—Gwen, Dr. Heckler, Arnold, Palmer. Perhaps I simply had not tried hard enough, had not given of myself freely.

"Sloan, if I'd known you wanted truth, I would have written it differently."

"I should hope so."

"We'll just change it to, 'Rooty-Tooties taste like absolute shit.' There you go. Kids all across the nation will be singing that jingle in their sleep."

He threw the copy on my desk and slammed my office door behind him.

I can change. It isn't too late. More time for my wife, the kids. I picked up the phone and made reservations at Orsini's and called it an early day.

We do not own a Lincoln MKX. So why was there one parked in our garage? The tarantula slithered up from my subconscious. It whispered, "Cuckold. Fat bastard."

I let myself in and climbed the stairs, weaving my web noiselessly, patiently. Sitting on the edge of our bed beside my wife was Dr. Heckler, his trousers collapsed in a ruffled heap around his ankles.

"Mr. Lipschitz—I didn't expect you home quite so—"

I grabbed him by the scruff of his neck and simultaneously hoisted him up by his J. Garcia necktie. His face crimsoned, eyeballs bulged. I lunged him headfirst down the stairway and tightened my hold, snapping cartilage like Thanksgiving wishbones. In a low gutteral rasp, Dr. Heckler informed me, "I'm playing a *role*, Mr. Lipschitz, a *role!*"

"I know," I said. "You're about to play the role of an unfortunate victim."

Out the front door and into the air he went, falling bluntly upon the lawn in the glittering cascade of the automatic sprinkler system. Mrs. Lourdes across the street dropped the groceries she was unloading from her car and gawked.

"This is a positive development, Mr. Lipschitz," Dr. Heckler said, between coughing spasms. "You're jealous, which means you love your wife."

"No," I said. "I still hate her."

"Then why in the world would you *do* this to me?"

"Because I hate you more."

Captains may choose to go down with their ships, but there's no law that says civilians have to. The next day at the office I rang my secretary, Rebecca, and asked her to bring me the Yellow Pages. Blond, maturely graceful, Rebecca lit the room as she entered and placed the directory before me. Her tailored Liz Claiborne suit belied the firm trim waist it sought to cover. In her mid-thirties, one had to wonder why she had never married and raised a family. She caught me admiring the shape of her leg. She reddened.

"Is there anything else, Mr. Lipschitz?"

How strange, hearing that question from her, at that moment. *In life, Rebecca, besides you, is there anything else—that might make me happy? That may make me feel whole again? That would allow me to feel less like a failure, a fat bastard?*

The answer rang out like a clarion, with the purity truth always carries: "No."

Lawn mowers . . . Lawyers—ah, there they were. About twenty thousand of them. I ran my finger down the column indiscriminately and stopped at Benjamin, Jeffrey. He sounded vaguely patriotic, stalwart, like someone you could count on to make it through a thunderstorm, kite intact.

Later at his office, I poured my heart out to him, a complete stranger, telling tales of cruelty beyond imagination. Jeffrey Benjamin, clean-shaven, bespectacled, paced across his hand-woven Lebanese carpet, hands clasped behind his back. A little tuft of hair stranded between two isthmuses of smooth, bald scalp had been perfectly combed in place. He shook his head, crestfallen.

"Fifty-seven percent, Mr. Lipschitz. That's how many marriages fail in this country. Did you know that?"

"Let's shoot for fifty-eight." Rebecca pirouetted across my thoughts like a corporate ballerina.

He sat tentatively upon his black lacquered Thayer-Coggin desk, his hands riding the razor-sharp creases of his trousers. "People are no longer prepared to go the distance."

"What do you mean?" I asked.

"The *distance*, Mr. Lipschitz, the *distance*. Everybody wants an easy way out. Any other contract is more airtight, more sacrosanct than a matrimonial agreement."

Perhaps the Yellow Pages had been a poor lead. I said, "Are you sure you're a lawyer?"

He stood up and looped a finger in the buttonhole of his Hart, Schaffner & Marx pinstripe suit coat. "'Till death do us part,'" he announced.

"Pardon?"

"That's what you agreed to when you married."

Death. The word pounced upon me like a rabid epiphany. It was right there in my marriage vows, in plain sight, but overlooked—a trap door.

"But I'm miserable," I said.

"How do you know you won't be more miserable alone?"

"I don't think that's possible."

He now walked alongside a floor-to-ceiling bookcase, tapping the spines of legal volumes as if they were chiropractic patients. "I didn't think it was possible, either." He cast a longing glance at a framed family portrait on the far wall: two grinning kids, a decidedly less-grinning woman, and himself, before the ravaged hairline. "Don't misunderstand me, Mr. Lipschitz. I'll represent you in a divorce proceeding, if you're sure that's what you want. But do you know how your economic lifestyle will change?"

"Let me guess. She'll get everything and I'll be broke."

He spun around like a dervish from his bookcase vantage point. "*No*. You'll *both* be broke, relatively speaking. And your children will become commuting visitors."

Till death do us part, I thought.

"Makes you think," he said, "doesn't it?"

"Yes. It makes me think."

Death.

Jeffrey Benjamin strode slowly back to his desk on legs that reminded me of fat *kishkes*. He reached into the breast pocket of his suit coat and produced a box of Rooty-Tooties. He opened it, poured some in his open palm, and said, "Have you considered marriage counseling?"

Gwen and I stayed together for the children.

That is not true. That's just what I tell people. We stayed together so I could afford my new BMW Sportster and so she could continue her quest to empty out Neiman Marcus on a weekly basis.

I don't want you to think that I was an innocent party. I struck back if for no other reason than to maintain a shabby sense of self-respect. For instance, one night I sneaked upstairs to her closet and removed three stitches from the seat of every pair of slacks she owned. I replaced her nail polish remover with Crazy Glue. And I once flirted with the notion of turning her in as the Zodiac Killer, but neither the police nor I had any evidence. But all of that was nothing compared to the dark secret visions that had begun to fester within my mind: Gwen, a meat cleaver firmly imbedded in her skull, or else hanging in her closet, suspended from the light fixture on the ceiling by the improvised noose of a Donna Karan belt. I could not stop these thoughts. It was all Jeffrey Benjamin's fault.

At some point, desire gave way to action. It was inevitable. One autumn afternoon when the leaves caromed down the streets and the wild scent of possibility perfumed the air, Rebecca brushed up against me at the water cooler. Thigh upon thigh, our eyes met; a burgeoning sensation boiled in my loins, and I held her by the arms tightly, briefly.

That was the weekend I was to take Arnold and Palmer camping. I wanted to know my sons man-to-man, to have a hand in shaping the adults they would become, and to get as far away from Gwen as possible. Up in the bedroom I tossed a few last minute necessities in my backpack—mosquito repellent, jackknife, a copy of *Swank* I'd been saving—when I stepped on something hard just beneath the dust ruffle of the bed. A key ring—not mine. I picked it up and examined the embossed monogram—*NH*. Unless my wife was sleeping with Nathaniel Hawthorne, odds were it belonged to Dr. Norton Heckler—playing the role of a suburban Casanova. And I knew what Gwen must have been secretly thinking: *He'll never know. He'll be upstate in a tent, the fat bastard.*

Rage seethed throughout the sinews of my chest, beneath what I admit to be a layer of glyceride ester. But it was genuine rage, no matter how far down there it was. Arnold interrupted the heinous impulses that stormed my brain like a cavalry regiment.

"Dad, where's the flashlight?"

Backpack thrown over my shoulder, saliva thick in my mouth, I went to the basement and kicked my way past picnic coolers and a croquet set no one had ever used. I bent over to pick up the Coleman flashlight and cracked my head hard on the gas line that fed the furnace. The reverberation could be heard the length of the pipe, right to the valve joint, a joint, it occurred to me, that could easily be loosened, flooding the entire house with silent, stalking natural gas. I'd be a widower. Neighbor women would pity me and bring casseroles over. The house, the kids, Gwen's insurance money—all mine. The wrench hung on the pegboard before me, temptingly, alluringly. The warm musculature of Rebecca's thigh was fresh within my memory. A wishful twist of the joint, that's all it required.

The boys were on their fifty-seventh verse of "Ninety-nine Bottles of Beer on the Wall" as we sped past meadows and copses, livestock, silos, ploughed furrows, and abandoned lean-tos. I approximated the progress of the gas fumes, weaving their facile way through air ducts and under doorways, invisible, deadly.

Ah, nature! For the next two days it surrounded my sons and me, coddled and caressed us. We breathed freely. There were no harsh words or worries. The earth, sweet mother, nestled us close to her bosom and we slept upon her dreamlessly.

And on the return trip I reveled in visions of Gwen snapping on a light switch, and the apocalyptic explosion that would follow—the roof blown to high heaven, windows shattered, a fusillade of shrapnel raining helter-skelter; a conflagration of Spielberg-esque proportions, orange and russet flames spewing upward, licking the sky; plumes of noxious smoke, billowing black cumulus clouds blooming convulsively like dark roses in time-lapse photography, consuming all—air, trees, adjoining lots; a miniature and localized nuclear winter, sprinkling pellets of glass over hedges and tool sheds, fences and lawns. They could rename the subdivision *Dresden Estates.*

As I negotiated the turn onto our block, the station wagon lumbering down the quiet street, I found no charred brickwork, no debris or detritus. The house sat undamaged. A jolt of adrenaline sent my carotid artery into palpitating paradiddles as I pictured Gwen rigid upon the floor, pale blue and white, the color of an overcast sky.

"I'm itchy," Palmer said, his face a Baedeker of red splotches and welts.

In place of my son I found a human rash, a billboard ad for Caladryl.

"Jesus Christ, what happened to you?"

Just then the front door exploded open and out jumped Gwen, clad in Calvin Klein leotards, fresh from her step-aerobics class. She had never looked healthier, more unsettlingly alive. The daydream of the loosened gas valve dissolved under the harsh light of reality. It existed only in the twisted playground of my mind.

"What did you do with those keys?" she demanded of me. The caviling had begun already.

"What keys?" I answered, innocently.

"You took them deliberately, didn't you? He can't get into his office, he can't start his car—" She suddenly raised a hand to her mouth and let out a slight gasp that sounded like, "Huh!" Arnold and his brother the blister stepped out of the car. "Poison ivy! What have you done to my baby? You call yourself a father? You call yourself a man? You're not a man. You're a—"

Let's say it in unison: —*"fat bastard!"*

Mrs. Lourdes, hands on her saggy hips, witnessed my tongue lashing with relish from across the street. Her cable TV must have been on the blink. I slunk into the house and retreated to the relative safety of the den, defeated again. I allowed myself the private victory of flushing Heckler's keys down the toilet in the adjoining bathroom, but it brought me little joy.

Monday morning I sat at my desk at Hirsch and Bristol and pondered my marriage. Should it come as a surprise that something once beautiful had decayed into vulgarity and ugliness? Consider a bouquet of flowers. Freshly picked, they are lovely, inspirational. Smell the vase water a week later—rank, fetid, not unlike living with Gwen.

When Rebecca cornered me again at the water cooler, pressing her sumptuous breast against my arm, I crushed my Dixie Cup, tossed it in the wastebasket, and said, "What's the point?"

She looked hurt, poor thing. But it was too late. I had yielded— to life, to marriage, to writing wholesome and vapid copy for Rooty- Tooties and their subsidiary cousins, Crunchy-Bunchies and Zingy- Dingies.

Yielding, however, came with its rewards. It rendered Gwen's ego-piercing insults harmless. Words like *fat* packed no more wallop than *buff*. I came to look upon the other weapons in her verbal arsenal as low forms of endearment. This new approach lowered my blood pressure, saved me from my ulcer, and had the additional advantage of driving Gwen nuts. For example, when I recently asked her to please not park her Volvo so close to my BMW, because her driver's side door was leaving nicks in the paint finish, she came at me with guns blazing.

"Listen, fatso, is that supposed to be criticism?"

"No, dear."

"Are you trying to tell me how to park?"

"Of course not, darling."

"You just better watch it, lard-ass."

"I will."

She balled up her fists, kicked an ottoman, and left the den in a huff. I sat back in my recliner calmly and finished reading the sports page, cool as a new pickle.

Three days ago while sitting at my desk, perusing a print ad for a popular antacid, I was still basking in the afterglow of my subtle concession revelation. Unexpectedly, from the narrow open crevice of my office door, I spied Sloan Dovedale and Rebecca at the water cooler. She moved her school-girl soft thigh along the inseam of Sloan's slacks. He reciprocated by cupping her buttocks. I thought about this all the way home on the commuter line. *Perhaps they will marry and drive each other to the brink of insanity,* I thought. I certainly hoped so. And then I recalled that this was the night I was to drive Arnold to the seventh grade social, his first dance, his introduction to the gender game. For a moment I worried about him, wondered what inflated expectations filled his head. Then Rebecca's thigh grazed my field of consciousness as the train teetered and hurled down the track.

I was struck dumb as Arnold descended the stairs. Gone were the baggy shorts and baseball cap. In their place—a Gucci jacket, Givenchy contrasting-collared shirt, pleated Dockers. Every hair was blown-dry and gelled in place. This was not my son; this was George Clooney. And what was that smell? Christian Dior Eau Sauvage—a couple hundred liters of it. He was flammable, but elegant.

"*Look* at *you*," I said.

"C'mon, Dad. Let's just go."

I swelled with pride as I admired him—but the moment was spoiled. I sensed a dark presence lurking behind me. I have developed Gwen radar.

"I hope you remembered that this Saturday is my cousin Lilly's wedding."

I did not even remember that she *had* a cousin Lilly. "Gosh, I'm sorry," I said, turning to face her, "but this weekend I have the Sawyer Invitational Tournament. Sawyer's a big account."

"Do you mean to tell me you're going to snub my family for some stupid golf match?"

That was what I was trying *not* to tell her.

"Dad," Arnold pleaded, "c'mon!"

I chose that moment to make my escape, but Gwen followed us to the foyer. She reached in her purse and then dangled her car keys toward me at arm's length. Arnold, she informed me, had a date. "You won't all fit in that hot rod of yours," she added, caustically.

"It's not a hot rod. It's a *sportster*."

A murderous cloud slid across the horizon of Gwen's face. She leaned in close to me and growled, "Cancel that golf match, or you'll be sorry you didn't."

My blood turned to Freon. Something in her tone, in the serrated blade of her voice, cut at me with surgical precision.

◆

"We have to pick up Nicky."

"Who?"

"Nicky. Nicky *Hensen*. I promised we'd give him a ride." This was Grace, Arnold's date, a darling little girl who had been named for the one characteristic she did not possess.

"But I thought you were going to the dance with Arnold," I said.

"I *am*. But I promised Nicky."

Nicky Hensen lived nine miles out of district, and from what I could gather, intended to crash the seventh grade social. He did not use the car door. He hopped in through the rear passenger window.

"Hey, babe," he said to Grace. "Whaddaya say, Schitz," he greeted Arnold.

Schitz. The name triggered painful memories. It was what I had been called in junior high.

I dropped the kids off and watched as they walked toward the line at the school entrance. Nicky—his straight blond hair parted down the middle, a surfer clone—dangled his arm around Grace's shoulders, shamelessly helping himself to my son's girl. Arnold trailed behind, biting urbanely at a hangnail. I shook my head, relieved that I would not have to witness the rest of their evening.

I did not want to go home, dreaded what awaited me, so for the next three and a half hours I sat in the station wagon and gazed at the lambent gymnasium windows while the *thump-thump-thump* of staccato bass lines rocked my ulcer. Stars were born, swathed in the evening gloam. Leaves rustled wistfully at one another. Puddles reflected streetlights upon the macadam. The car phone rang.

Should I answer it? Who calls Gwen at this hour? Neiman Marcus? Nordstrom? Norton Heckler?

"Hello?"

"Did you cancel the golf outing?"

A breeze stirred outside the car window. The leaves hissed and snarled. I swallowed hard. "Gwen, I told you. Sawyer's a big account."

A low grating moan—or was it a laugh? "All right. Remember,

I warned you. You'll be sorry."

"Look," I said, "it's out of my—hello? Gwen?"

She hung up. I slowly eased the phone away from my ear. *She's bluffing,* I thought. *How much sorrier could I be?* Soon the school doors heaved open and the entire seventh grade class plus one spilled into the night. My eyes sifted the crowd expectantly. Hordes of adolescents hooted and yammered pubescent inanities. Car doors opened and shut; headlights floated away. When the crowd had thinned to almost nothing, three silhouettes hobbled haltingly toward the car, like refugees. Panic tightened my gullet. I recognized Arnold first, hands held tightly behind his back as he seesawed from one leg to the other. Behind him was Grace, a shoe in her hand, a bandage wrapped around her foot. And at Grace's side, supporting her with an arm around her waist—Nicky Hensen, looking as though he had just been invented by MTV.

I shot out of the car. "Are you kids all right? What happened?

"You should've seen it!" Nicky raved, his long California hair swinging metronomically against his face. "It was way-cool, awesome. Schitz ripped his pants doin' the limbo. Split 'em right up the middle, and at first he didn't even know, and he's like, 'What's everybody lookin' at?' You could see his boxers. *Polka* dots! And then he slow dances with Grace and she starts screamin' like crazy and all the teachers and stuff come runnin' and they put Grace on a stretcher and carry her to the nurse's office and—"

"Nicky," I interrupted, "just tell me what happened to her."

"Schitz stepped on her foot."

"I think I'm dying," Grace whimpered.

Arnold hung his head, attempting desperately to bear the weight of his humiliation. My poor boy. I longed to comfort him, to hand him back his self-respect, reassembled, if only I knew how.

"You *dweeb!*" Grace surprised me. She had recovered enough to spit venom. "You did it on purpose!"

Arnold's head shot up. His eyes, like escaped prisoners, ran back and forth between me and his accuser, as if searching for a place to hide. "No," he said. "No, I . . . it was an accident."

I could take no more of this. "All right, kids. Let's get in the car.

It's getting—"

"Don't gimme that! Nobody's *that* clumsy. You did it 'cause I told you what a rotten dancer you are."

Arnold seemed to be getting smaller, as if he were shrinking into himself. *Don't take it,* I thought. *Defend yourself. Don't let anyone do this to you.* But he remained mute, deflated. He only had eyes for the pavement.

"Ow, I think I'm dying," Grace reminded us.

I turned off the engine and killed the headlights. The two of us sat in the station wagon out on the driveway in embarrassed silence. From our open windows I could hear the mournful song of a cricket out of season. My son stared straight ahead through the windshield at nothing. He did not move. He did not even blink. From somewhere deep within his being he managed to extract the words, "It was an accident. I promise."

"I know," I said. The cricket stopped, as if the better to hear us. "You know, someday you'll look back on this and—"

Arnold turned and looked at me as if I had lost my mind.

"—laugh."

It was a lie, and he knew it was a lie. He would feel the sting of his failure for the rest of his life, at odd moments of introspection— standing in line at a movie theater, or deep in the heart of a sleepless night, cut off from the world by darkness and solitude.

"Dad?"

"Hm?"

"Can I go to a different school?"

I grasped his shoulder and squeezed it. Even his bones beneath the blazer felt somehow diminished. "We'll talk about it in the morning."

He opened the car door and I watched him waddle awkwardly to the house, still holding the split seam of his pants. It was a pitiful sight.

I restarted the motor and pushed the remote control button. Light spilled from beneath the automatic door as it ascended. I reached for the gearshift, but my arm fell limp. What I saw could not be real.

I staggered from the station wagon and up the drive toward the heap of twisted metal imbedded in the inner brick wall of the garage. It lay before me inert, battered, a palsied creature. I glazed my hand over accordion-like ripples of contorted steel, stroked the scars of the creased fender, the crumpled trunk lid. Abrasions and contusions marred the shredded side molding; lacerations spider-webbed the curvilinear surfaces of windows. Shattered red plastic fragments that had once been brake lights crunched beneath my shoes, and the optional magnesium racing wheels were now collapsed inwardly like club feet. Traumatized, wantonly violated, savagely beaten, its life slowly trickled out of it in a slick-thick pool of antifreeze—my sportster, my BMW. I fell to my knees and embraced what was left of the freely hanging bumper. Gwen had gone too far this time.

I don't know how long I was out there grieving my loss, my *losses*, for certainly they were more than the sum of the parts of the car. But I *do* know that when I went back into the house I was several steps over the line of rationality. Madness possessed me. What else could explain what I set out to do? Sane men do not strangle their wives in their sleep.

I quietly climbed the staircase and peeked in on Arnold and Palmer. Both were out; it was a z-fest in there. Sleep had granted my oldest boy a temporary reprieve from his first romantic failure, a failure I would, in my own way, avenge soon. I pulled the bedroom door to and tiptoed down the hall. All was quiet; all was dark, except for the meager glow of the night light in the room where the beast slept. I entered, stealthy as a mouser. I listened: nothing but the well-regulated slow and easy rise and fall of breath. She would die in her sleep, or else take with her to eternity a last mortal glimpse of me upon her, teeth gritted, wringing the tissue of her esophagus to pulp.

I padded gently to the bed, cautious not to creak a floorboard, and eased my way onto the mattress. She made no movement. I sidled up to her sleeping form from behind; she was on her side, facing away from me. All the better. She was nothing more than an evil outline, a maumet, cloaked in shadows. I wiped the perspiration from my hands on the bed quilt and reached one of them carefully under her neck, and closed the other over the skin of her warm throat, her pulse just palpable upon my fingertips. It surely was this that disturbed her. All at once she turned over on her back as I whisked my hands away, tucking them beneath the covers like guilty co-conspirators. But she slept on, eyelids closed, her face now bathed in the yellow beam of the night light. Devoid of expression, transcendent, nearly angelic, her face was—the way it appeared to me when first I saw it, that sunlit day at the harbor. Unconsciousness had lifted the veil and restored her beauty. I remembered her smile on our honeymoon when we walked hand-in-hand on the burning white sand of Captiva Island, how the world seemed to open up, soft and new and fresh, as though it had been created just for us, a tropical paradise. Playing in the waves, dancing after dinner, the soft Gulf Stream breeze lifting her hair. . . .

I lay my head down upon my pillow and watched her, thinking all this, you see, thinking of the way we used to be so many years ago when our youthful dreams were still alive, when we were in love and innocent and happy, until I fell softly, soundly into blissful sleep.

Acknowledgments

The following stories in this collection have been published previously:

"Connecticut Holiday"—*Story Quarterly*

"Where People Go" —*World Wide Writers*

"Till Death Do Us Part" (under the title "Going the Distance") —*World Wide Writers*

Greg Herriges began writing professionally in his twenties with an investigative report on gangs for The *Chicago Tribune* Magazine, "Inherit the Streets." Soon afterward, he met with his literary hero, J.D. Salinger at Salinger's home in Cornish, New Hampshire, a meeting that resulted in his first national publication, a profile/interview with the iconic author. It inspired Herriges to turn to fiction writing, and years later was the subject of his book-length *JD: A Memoir of a Time and a Journey* (Wordcraft of Oregon, 2006).

He is the author of novels, short stories, and articles, as well as a series of literary DVD documentaries, including *Thomas E. Kennedy: Copenhagen Quartet*, and the award winning *TC Boyle: The Art of the Story.*

His short works have appeared in *Story Quarterly, The Literary Review, The South Carolina Review, The Encyclopedia of Beat Literature,* and Great Britain's *Popular Music and Society* and *World Wide Writers.*

His new ebook novels *Streethearts* and *Lennon and Me* are available in ebook shops everywhere.

He is currently a professor of English at William Rainey Harper College in Palatine, Illinois.

Made in the USA
Charleston, SC
20 September 2011